Underground River and Other Stories

Inés Arredondo

Translated by Cynthia Steele
With a foreword by Elena Poniatowska

University of Nebraska Press
Lincoln and London

These stories originally
appeared in Spanish in Inés
Arredondo's *Obras completas*
(Mexico City: Siglo XXI, 1989).

© 1996 by the University
of Nebraska Press

Library of Congress
Cataloging-in-Publication Data

Arredondo, Inés.
[Selections. English]
Underground river and other
stories / Inés Arredondo;
translated by Cynthia Steele;
with a foreword by Elena
Poniatowska.
p.   cm. — (Latin American
women writers)
ISBN 0-8032-1034-5
(cloth: alk. paper)
1. Arredondo, Inés—
Translations into English.
I. Steele, Cynthia. II. Title.
III. Series.
PQ7298.1.R7A27   1996
863–dc20   95-37585   CIP

Photo of the author (page i)
by Rogelio Cuéllar.

Contents

Introduction

Cynthia Steele

Inés Arredondo (1928–1989) was the most important Mexican woman short-story writer of the twentieth century. She published just three slim volumes of stories over a period of twenty-three years, yet her reputation as a great writer, "a necessary writer," is firmly established in Mexico. Her works dwell on a few central obsessions: erotic love, evil, purity, perversion, prostitution, tragic separation, and death. Most of her characters are involved in ill-fated searches for the absolute, through both excessively passionate and sadomasochistic relationships. Inevitably the perfect, pure dyad of two youthful lovers is interrupted or corrupted, through the interference of a third party (a rival lover or a child—"Great lovers don't have children"), aging, death, or public morality (in the cases of incest and homosexuality). Time and again, excess—whether of love, passion, possessiveness, or narcissism—has tragic consequences for both the lovers and the innocent people around them.

Many of Arredondo's stories are set in the great

house of a hacienda in Sinaloa, a tropical state in northwest Mexico. The regal house and sumptuous orchards are based loosely on Arredondo's memories of Eldorado, the suggestively named sugarcane plantation (named after that legendary city of gold sought by the Spanish conquistadores) where her grandfather was the overseer and where she spent her summers, the happiest part of her childhood, with him and her grandmother:[2]

> The hacienda took up many thousands of acres, and all the roads were lined with guava trees. The village and the sugar mill are circumscribed by miles and miles of orchards; orchards of litchis brought from China, of *cuadrado* trees from India, of star-apple trees from Peru, of medlars from Japan, of pineapple-mangos, guava-mangos, pear-mangos. Orchards with the only Chinese people in Sinaloa who hadn't been deported in the times of President Calles, and who kept right on patiently constructing their mosaics of vegetables and talking about the express boat from Peking. Orchards containing enormous cages of birds brought from all over the world; cool canals that widened out into swimming pools lined by Doric columns, and then ran along the avenues shaded by bamboo.
>
> Eldorado was created, built, tree by tree and shadow upon shadow. Two madmen, father and son, over two generations, invented a scenery, a town, and a way of life. My grandfather was an accomplice to them both, and he laid out and sowed with his own hands the orchards that I believed had always been there. He dedicated his whole life to achieving the invented reality that I lived. And that was made for that purpose, to be lived and not

---

[2]Inés's maternal grandfather, Francisco Arredondo, the overseer on Eldorado, was really her great-uncle. She took his last name, Arredondo, as her pen name. (In so doing, she in effect usurped her mother's name, even as she assumed the older woman's memories for her works.) She also named two of her children after these adopted grandparents, and the third after herself, thus recreating the happy fictive family of her childhood.

to be made into literature, I know. But when I use that reality, it is with the awareness that it has a real weight of its own, aside from what it might have in my experience.

My grandfather, over six feet tall and enormously serious, went around dressed like an Englishman in the colonies: white linen, leather leggings, and a caftan. But that apparel, which anywhere else would have been a costume, was the appropriate dress for Eldorado, by virtue of the simple fact that it was the chosen one. Not long ago—after my grandfather had died and all my children had been born—I discovered that nowhere in Mexico did people dress like that, or live that way, or want that fundamental thing that people in Eldorado wanted: the luxury of *creating*, not the luxury of *having*, of *creating a way of life*.

And so I grew up surrounded by trees and birds that I thought were mine, the cockatoo as much as the sparrow: irremediably mine. But you can see that, since birth, I'm not made to believe in determinisms, not even geographical ones. To me, the Australian parakeets and the flamingos in the midst of the immense orchards were not only natural, but nature itself.

(Arredondo, *Obras* 3–4)

Eldorado still stands, in ruins, outside the city of Culiacán; the great house is now used as a luxury hunting lodge. Before Inés's time, the house had held an enormous aviary that took up an entire floor and was filled with rare birds from around the world, like the one portrayed in "The Nocturnal Butterflies." According to Arredondo's mother and sister, Inés never saw this but knew about it from family stories. This and many of the other aristocratic and exotic trappings in her stories belong to her mother's childhood memories, rather than her own (personal interview with Inés Arredondo Cevallos and Rosa Camelo, Mexico City, 16 July 1991).

Just as she refers to the creation of Eldorado, and the selection of British colonial attire that would have seemed ridiculous anywhere else in Mexico, Arredondo often spoke and wrote of the lives that we choose, that she found so much more intriguing than those we are born into. It seems clear, from her description, that part of the nostalgia apparent in her work is for a colonial social order, not unlike Southern plantation life in the United States. In the same autobiographical essay, she anticipates accusations that she is adopting a reactionary political position. Growing up under the affectionate tutelage of the cowhands and farmworkers, she argues, "made me think it natural that they later became the owners of the land, for the simple reason that they were the ones who truly possessed it. I learned the idea of poor trash, of the mob, of dirty Indians, many years later, precisely in the pages of Mexican literature" (Arredondo, *Obras* 6).

She identified two happy periods in her own life, childhood and adolescence. Of the childhoods available to her, she chose particular aspects of her early years in Culiacán, in the tropical coastal region of the western Mexican state of Sinaloa.

For the most part, Arredondo's memories of growing up in the state capital were unhappy ones: "In Culiacán, in school, with my parents, I felt embedded in a vast, foreign reality, that seemed shapeless to me. On the other hand, in Eldorado, the existence of a basic order made it possible to become a harmonic element at the very moment that one accepted that order. In Eldorado it was demonstrated that, if creation was the work of madmen, then madmen were right" (Arredondo, *Obras* 3). In Culiacán, Inés's family lived in a roomy house that doubled as a doctor's office for her father's obstetrics-gynecology practice. It sat right off the main square, with an ice cream parlor on one corner and a flame tree on another. This setting provided a perfect vantage point for observing the daily life and public ceremonies of the provincial capital. As a child, she remembers eating guava sherbet under the flame tree, while her father recited from memory the *Romancero del Cid*, a popular Spanish ballad about El Cid, the medieval hero:

> Among them there rides Rodrigo,
> the proud Castilian.
> They're all mounted on mules,
> only Rodrigo rides a horse;
> they're all dressed in gold and silver,
> Rodrigo is well armed.
> . . . .

they all wear such fine hats,
Rodrigo an elegant helmet,
and on top of the helmet he wears
a bright red bonnet.

"On horseback, armed, different from the rest, the absolute hero,
Ruy Díaz made me laugh with the peculiar extravagance of his
bright red bonnet. . . . That bonnet," writes Arredondo, "represents what isn't epic, a sign of what is personal in the Cid, something
nostalgic, in tatters, linked to the land, to his land . . . my first
contact with the idea of irony, which I later found formulated in
Kierkegaard, and which is so important to my life and works, took
place at age six, when I laughed at that bright red bonnet of the
Cid's" (Arredondo, *Obras* 5). These early recitations awakened in
the author a hunger for books, like the one that propels the female
protagonist in "The Nocturnal Butterflies."

During the Mexican Revolution (1910–20), Arredondo's
father had been an official in the army of de la Huerta and had
served as governor of the southeastern state of Campeche for a few
days or weeks. Family lore has it that, forced to flee when Huerta
was defeated, he had stowed away on a steamship headed from
Veracruz to Cuba, dressed as a woman. He had later returned
home with a seemingly endless repertoire of Cuban songs (personal
interview with the author, Mexico City, May 1989).

During the Spanish Civil War (1936–40), most resi-
dents of conservative, provincial Culiacán supported the fascists.
Arredondo, however, followed attentively as her father, a leftist,
listened to the radio news and plotted the progress of the Repub-
lican forces on a wall map. (In 1952, she would witness a stirring
speech by the socialist presidential candidate, Vicente Lombardo
Toledano, on the same square where she used to eat sherbet and
fantasize about knights-errant.) In spite of these happy childhood
memories of politics, literature, and family legends, Arredondo
described herself as a sickly, withdrawn, solitary child. She was
afraid of her two little brothers, was not close to her four younger
sisters, and had a very distant relationship with her mother, a society matron active in the Catholic Ladies Association. Like most
middle-class Mexican children, Inés was raised by a nanny, who
taught her to sew and knit. Years later, this training allowed her

to support her husband and children by running a handmade-clothing shop in Mexico City. Later, she went on to earn a master's degree in literature from the Autonomous National University, and to work in the university's public relations office.

The author's first marriage, to the exiled Spanish poet Tomás Segovia, with whom she had three children, was an unhappy one. She began writing short fiction as a form of self-therapy after another child, which would have been her second, was stillborn. She described her second marriage, to Dr. Carlos Ruiz Sánchez, as "immensely happy." Yet the last decade of her life was marred by the pain and isolation brought on by a lengthy illness: chronic back problems entailing several painful and unsuccessful operations.

Although Arredondo lived her entire adult life in Mexico City (except for a two-year sojourn in Uruguay), nearly all of her stories are set in the Sinaloa of her childhood, several of them on the Eldorado plantation. Along with the lush tropical setting, the fairytale flora and fauna, she emphasizes the oppressive aspects of the staunchly Roman Catholic, patriarchal social structure.

Arredondo resisted being called a woman writer, since she believed that this label relegated women artists to a ghetto, to a second-class status with critics and readers. "I don't want to be the best woman writer in Mexico," she said in an interview, "I want to be one of the best Mexican writers." At the same time, her short stories focus obsessively on female subjectivity (along with that of other marginal beings, adolescents of both genders and gay men) within the context of a perverse Gothic "family romance" set in provincial Sinaloa at the beginning of the twentieth century. The Revolution has not yet happened, or else it has passed through without disturbing centuries-old power relations.

Her adult male characters are often predators, depraved collectors of adolescent virgins, like the plantation owners in "The Nocturnal Butterflies" and "Shadow in the Shadows," or the dying uncle in "The Shunammite," who is kept alive by incestuous lust. Since the young female protagonists almost never have fathers to protect them, the only people to stand between them and these lechers are older women, mothers or aunts. Yet the latter usually betray their young charges, satisfying their own lust for money by acting as go-betweens or procurers. The mother in "The Nocturnal Butterflies," for instance, sells her daughter to a man who has "a reputation for being a depraved lecher" in exchange for gaining access to wealth and power through her daughter's marriage; the perverse suitor slyly courts the mother in order to procure the daughter. In these stories, older women are accomplices in the sordid, age-old traffic in women, as are the extended family and the Roman Catholic Church.

This traffic also extends to children. For instance, in "The Mirrors" (which, according to José de la Colina, reads like the Mexican equivalent of a spaghetti Western), the narrator resents her daughter-in-law for not giving her a grandchild. When finally she complies and, predictably, proves to be an unfit mother, the older woman considers it her duty to take the child away from her daughter-in-law. All the representatives of patriarchy—the older woman's husband, a wealthy landowner; her son, the baby's father; and the family doctor—support her decision. This female rivalry over control of the next generation sets in motion a series of shocking events that are worthy of Greek tragedy. (Not surprisingly, the bad mother is named Isis, and she is based on the author's real maternal grandmother—as opposed to the great aunt that she called her grandmother, Isabel Ibarra de Arredondo, wife of the Eldorado overseer.)

Both "The Nocturnal Butterflies" and "Shadow in the Shadows" portray innocent young women literally bought (as wives or mistresses) by wealthy lechers. Similar as they are thematically, these two stories however serve as point and counterpoint in their representation of female agency. In the latter story, the female protagonist surrenders to her husband's perversity, bringing on her own complete isolation and degeneration. In the former, the protagonist, a poor schoolteacher, assents to being sexually exploited in exchange for gaining access to European elite culture, in the form of books, paintings, and travel to Europe and Asia; when, however, the moment arrives for her exploiter to convert her into yet another art object for his collection, she walks away, taking with her only her newly acquired knowledge.

The most frequent outcome for Arredondo's characters, both female and male, is for them to be driven to self-degradation and madness, in their futile but necessary search for the sign that will reveal the meaning of existence to them. They experience fleeting moments of ecstasy in which they catch a glimpse of this meaning, but it can never be grasped or retained. In "The Sign," the protagonist's revelation consists of the knowledge that he has experienced something transcendental that he will never understand. In "Mariana," a character kills the woman he loves because he cannot share her raptures, then goes insane. Mariana, for her part, had fruitlessly searched for her husband-murderer's spirit in other men's bodies; she was unable to recognize the capacity for transcendence within herself that drove her husband mad when he could not possess and control it.

Arredondo wrote sparingly, publishing little more than thirty short stories in twenty-three years. She once told an interviewer that she waited for the holy ghost to spit on her as a sign that she should write a new story; but since he was a ghost, he didn't have much saliva. She told me that one of her most enigmatic stories, "The Brothers," a dreamlike reflection on passion, female virginity, and male honor, was dictated to her by a voice in the shower. "Shadow in the Shadows," in which she explored every conceivable sort of sexual perversion in order to demonstrate the impossibility of distinguishing between purity and prostitution, came to her as she sat sipping coffee under the arches on the idyllic main plaza in Oaxaca.

What these disembodied voices offered Arredondo was a key phrase that helped her to establish the tone; once the tone was established, she claimed, the story would practically write itself. Perhaps this explains why, as Juan José Reyes has pointed out, her openings are so memorable:

> That was a blistering summer, the last of my youth. ("The Shunammite")

> The dense, immobile sun imposed its presence; reality was paralyzed under its cruelty without respite. ("The Sign")

> Great lovers don't have children. ("On Love")

Other stories are based on tales that Arredondo heard from family and friends. "Mariana" is based on the story of a crime of passion that someone told her when she was twelve years old, and that she didn't understand until she wrote it down and turned it into a short story years later. Similarly, she fashioned "Underground River" after a story she had heard about three adult brothers and a sister, all of them mad, who lived in the town of Mocorito, Sinaloa, in a house with a staircase leading down to the river's edge. Today, the old building (which in reality is less grand than in the story) houses the Casa de la Cultura, a government arts center.

Despite the brevity of Arredondo's work, her elegant, crystalline style and her disturbing, highly original vision of the human condition, and of gender and power relations in northern Mexico at the beginning of the twentieth century, establish her as one of contemporary Mexico's most significant authors.

Inés Arredondo, Elena Poniatowska, and I selected the stories for this collection just two months before the author's sudden death from a heart attack on 2 November 1989. Subsequently I added one more story, "Orphanhood," to the original eleven.

Sources

Arredondo, Inés. *Obras completas.* Mexico City: Siglo XXI, 1989.

Reyes, Juan José. "La inminencia de los límites." *Casa del tiempo* 9.86 (June 1989): 37–38.

Foreword

Elena Poniatowska

Tall, very fair, her eyes somewhere between light brown and green, depending on how the light hit them, slender, Inés Arredondo realized very early that life could be a somber feast. She wanted to change everything, her name, her place of birth, and she didn't start to write until after her second child was born—stillborn. With her first short story, "The Quince Tree," she found out that she could write. A Northerner, born in Culiacán, Sinaloa—though she chose Eldorado as her birthplace—Inés the writer always had the sensation of "a bitter emptiness. It isn't anger, or spite, it's an emptiness." Despite Eldorado, legendary like the imaginary Mexico City five hundred years earlier (Gonzalo Aguirre went mad looking for the city invented by the Native Americans where everything was made of gold), Inés never gave the impression of being happy. Still, she recognized that Eldorado, "where the way of life was always being invented, one day at a time," was the most pleasant of her memories. The immense gardens, the fruit trees, the workers who would leave in flocks, all together on their bicycles, every evening at six—a neorrealist image to rival those of Italian cinema.

Inés didn't believe in happiness, nor did she find it in Mexico City, where she came to attend the university, at the urging of her grandfather, who paid for her studies and to whom she paid homage by taking the name Arredondo. "I learned the meaning of abject poverty when I came to this city. I learned this, and also that being Mexican was a terrible limitation in every sense: Teotihuacán excluded Chartres, Tenochtitlán excluded Florence, Cuauhtémoc excluded Cortés, Catholicism excluded liberalism, dark skin excluded light. As if that weren't bad enough, I found out that having been born in the Mexican Republic had made me hypocritical, melancholic, bloodthirsty and tender, sad and inferior. I shouldered this burden for a long time, much too long, but that doesn't mean that it forms part of my real history. For part of my good fortune was to have a liberal father, a supporter of de la Huerta, who nevertheless taught me that Spanish literature belonged to him and to me, just as much as the Revolution did."

Inés makes the following devastating judgment, with which I concurred for many years: "It seems to me that, in Mexico, everyone demands too little of themselves, and so they go bad very soon. When they've barely turned thirty, a 'someone' in Mexico is a lot less than that same person was at age twenty . . .

"If I believe it's possible in life to choose, out of the shapeless sum of events and actions that we live, those few and unique things with which one can interpret and make sense of life, I also believe that arranging actions on literary terrain is a discipline originating in another, more profound endeavor, in which the main problem is also the search for meaning. Not meaning in the sense of longing or direction or a goal, but in the sense of truth or presentiment of truth."

As for the young Inés Arredondo, the one who got married and with the exiled Spanish poet Tomás Segovia had three children, Inés, Ana Paula, and Francisco, the one who had many ontological problems in the department of philosophy and changed majors to devote herself to literature, I never knew her. I wonder whether Inés would have kept on inventing herself the way she invented her name and her biography.

As described by her, Culiacán can be unrecognizable. It is the city that she wished had existed. In Culiacán during the fifties, the director Juan Guerrero filmed a movie based on her short story "Mariana," and the two scriptwriters, Inés Arredondo and Juan García Ponce, traveled north for the filming. Also, the theater director Héctor Mendoza adapted "The Shunammite," a story that became famous from the moment it was published, for the movies.

With Tomás and their three children, Inés left for Montevideo, Uruguay, where they lived for two years. When they returned, Tomás and she got a divorce. During that period, I had not yet been able to make her acquaintance. I would hear people talk about her; that she was brilliant, extraordinarily sensitive, and that she slept a lot.

Finally, during the seventies, the journalist Margarita García Flores, a Northerner like her, took me to Gabriel Mancera Street to meet her. Inés was lying down, staring at the beams in the ceiling; she spoke with us from her bed. "I can't get up; I have low blood pressure." I was amazed by her critical capacity and her irony; everything she said was dazzling. A bedridden woman with such unusual strength, she trusted the character she had invented and named Inés Arredondo. She had faith and a great deal of confidence in herself. Inés's power went beyond what could be seen in the sickbed; she was the antithesis of self-pity. I didn't want to leave her side; what came out of her mouth enriched our world. Infinitely tender, open to others, generous, in that evocative voice she told us both:

"Friends, stop writing so many articles."

"So you read the newspapers, Inés?"

"I read everything."

Who was that figure lying there, propped up on oversized pillows in an oh-so-ordinary bed? In the semidarkness I tried to make out her smile, but my gaze kept bumping up against her long legs, her marble arms on top of the sheet, her hair spilling over the pillow.

I immediately read her short stories again: they have two readings, one for pleasure—perhaps even morbid pleasure—and a second, introspective reading that moves one to true reflection. Inés Arredondo is the most profound Mexican woman writer. It is difficult to find the same depth in other writers of our generation.

She was troubled by the problems of purity, pride, mercy, and love. Her central themes are reflected in her characters' solitude, in the importance that she confers on the couple, and in her dissection of the human soul; these are what make her works unique.

I went back to see her again and wrote down what she told me: "If the young people that study at the UNAM [National Autonomous University of Mexico] don't apply themselves, they'll end up being servants to those who study at the private universities, the Lasalle, the Iberoamericana, the Anahuac, the Monterrey Technological Institute. That's what Allende said in Guadalajara; the student's first obligation is to study."

For her thesis, *An Approach to Jorge Cuesta*, she chose the most hermetic, difficult, critical, desolate of poets, Jorge Cuesta. A biologist, as tormented as was she to find the meaning of our presence on this earth, being and nothingness, he shares her lucidity, her disillusionment.

Her first book, *The Sign*, published in 1965, was a great critical success. *Underground River*, published in 1979, was awarded the Xavier Villaurrutia Prize. In 1982, she finished her thesis on Cuesta, and she finally graduated in 1988. Her books were extremely well received by the critics, and many students are now closely analyzing Arredondo's works. The critics consider her to be the best Mexican woman writer of short stories. "The Shunammite" is one of the most celebrated short stories in Mexican literature, along with "Blame It on the Tlaxcaltecans," by Elena Garro, and "Death Has Permission," by Edmundo Valadés.

At one time, Inés was the soul and the goddess of the editorial board of the *Mexican Literary Journal*, although she didn't like cultural politics. As the only woman of her generation in the group, she had admirers: Huberto Batis and Juan García Ponce. A modest person, she never promoted herself, nor did she believe in publicity, but she did accept recognition in the form of praise from her readers.

Margarita, who had known her for years, confided in me that Inés went through periods of desperation, of anguish, intense depressions that caused her to fall into the hands of bad psychiatrists who made her worse. Alcohol is the best sedative. I've always been afraid of alcohol, because they say that Poles can't stop drinking: "drunk as a Polack." Inés felt in her bones the misfortunes of the world, which grew larger in private. Margarita used to joke with her, "Is that what you dedicate yourself to: suffering?" We're all neurotic.

From childhood, Inés was predisposed to illness, but her real health problems began with her divorce. They operated on her spinal column five times, and she was never cured. As a result, she was confined to a wheelchair for the rest of her life. Beginning in 1972, Dr. Carlos Ruiz Sánchez took charge of her care, and they got married. She was tended to by him and Justina, a totally dedicated young woman who would take her to Mexico Park to see the trees.

"I belong to a generation marked by calamities, a fucked-up generation; we were all unlucky, we're all in ruins. In this generation, you'll notice, there are the three Juans: Juan José Gurrola, Juan Vicente Melo, and Juan García Ponce; Salvador Elizondo; Huberto Batis, the only healthy one among us; Héctor Mendoza; José de la Colina; and Sergio Pitol, who saved himself by leaving Mexico and traveling around. All the rest of us have gone to pieces. Juan García Ponce, sick with his progressive paralysis that destroys the spinal cord, Juan Vicente Melo, sick with his alcoholism and lung cancer. Juan José Gurrola looks like 'Nosferatu,' running around on rooftops, flying around with his vampire's cape. The best thing to come out of Salvador Elizondo's pen is *Farabeuf*, which is about Chinese torture. Fernando García Ponce is dead. What more could possibly happen to us?"

Prematurely old, Inés lived to see the homage that her state, Sinaloa, paid her, although she had declared: "I detest Culiacán, I detest Sinaloans, who only value money. All of us from Culiacán are uncultured boors." She saw her complete works published by the Fondo de Cultura Económica and the government of Sinaloa.

When Cynthia Steele and I visited her, she demonstrated great enthusiasm for Cynthia's stupendous English translation of several of her short stories, and she spoke with us at great length, in that singular accent of hers. Cynthia Steele may have given her the last great joy in a life that had known so little happiness.

Inés Arredondo died at age sixty-one, on 2 November 1989.

(Translated by Cynthia Steele)

Underground River

and Other Stories

The Shunammite

So they sought for a fair damsel throughout all the coasts of Israel, and found Abishag a Shunammite, and brought her to the king, And the damsel was very fair and cherished the king and ministered to him: but the king knew her not.
—*I Kings 1:* iii–iv **AV**.

That was a blistering summer. The last of my youth.

Tensely concentrated in the defiance that precedes combustion, the city was burning in a single flame, dry and dazzling. In the center of the flame was I, dressed in black, proud, feeding the fire with my blonde tresses, alone. Men's gazes slid over my body without staining it, and my haughty reserve demanded that they speak to me with deference. I was certain I had the power to domesticate passions, to purify everything in the burning air that surrounded me without consuming me.

Nothing changed when I received the telegram; the sadness it brought on did not affect at all how I felt in the world: my Uncle Apolonio was dying at seventy-some years of age; he wanted to see me one last time, since I had lived in his house like a daughter for so long. I felt real sorrow at the prospect of that inevitable death. All of this was perfectly normal; no shudder, no foreboding made me suspect anything. Enveloped in the untouchable center of that ecstatic summer, I quickly made arrangements for the trip.

I arrived in town during the siesta.

Walking through the deserted streets clutching my little suitcase, I began to fall into the private dream of reality and time brought on by excessive heat. No, I did not remember it; I half-lived it, as I had then. "Look, Licha, the poppies are in bloom." The voice was clear, almost childlike. "For the sixteenth I want you to sew yourself a dress like Margarita Ibarra's." I heard her, felt her walking beside me, a bit stooped, light on her feet despite her girth, happy and old. I kept moving with my eyes half-closed, relishing my vague, tender anguish, sweetly submitting to the company of my Aunt Panchita, my mother's sister. "All right, dear, if you don't like Pepe ... but he isn't a bad boy." Yes, she had said that right here, under Tichi Valenzuela's window, with that delight of hers, innocent yet wicked. I walked a little farther, on sidewalk bricks now dull with age. When the bells chimed, heavy and real, marking the end of the siesta and calling people to the rosary, I opened my eyes and really looked at the town. It was different. The poppies had not bloomed; and there I stood in front of my uncle's house, weeping and dressed in mourning.

The gate was open, as usual, and at the back of the yard stood the bougainvillea tree. The same as ever. But not the same. I dried my tears, feeling more like I was saying good-bye than just arriving. Everything seemed static, as in memories, withered by the heat and silence. My footsteps echoed eerily as María came out to greet me.

"Why didn't you let us know you were coming? We would have sent ... "

We went straight to the sick man's room. As I walked in, I felt almost cold. The silence and darkness preceding death.

"Luisa, is it you?"

That fond voice was growing steadily softer and would soon fall silent altogether.

"Here I am, Uncle."

"Thank God; now I won't die alone."

"Don't say that; you'll be better in no time."

He smiled sadly, aware I was lying to him but not wanting to make me cry.

"Yes, Daughter, that's right. Now you rest, get settled in, and then come keep me company. I'm going to try to sleep a little."

He was smaller than before, toothless, shriveled up. He seemed lost in the enormous bed, floating senselessly on the drop of life he still had left. I felt tormented as if by the presence of something superfluous, out of place. So many dying people have this effect, which I recognized when I emerged into the steamy hallway and instinctively inhaled the light and air.

I started taking care of him and was content to do so. The house was *my* house and, on many mornings while I was straightening up, I would hum forgotten songs. The tranquility surrounding me may have derived from the fact that my uncle no longer awaited death as something imminent and terrible. Rather, he submitted to the days going by, to a shorter or longer future, with the oblivious sweetness of a child. He went over his life with pleasure and relished the idea of leaving his images in me, like grandparents do with their grandchildren.

"Bring me that little jewelry box that's up in the big closet. Yes, that one. The key's under the table cover, next to San Antonio; bring it, too."

And his sunken eyes revived at the sight of his treasures.

"Look, I gave this necklace to your aunt on our tenth wedding anniversary. I bought it in Mazatlán, from a Polish jeweler who told me some yarn about Austrian princesses and charged me an arm and a leg for it. I brought it home concealed in my holster, and I couldn't sleep a wink in the stagecoach, for fear someone might steal it from me ... "

Light from the setting sun set the young, vibrant stones sparkling in his arthritic hands.

"This ring with the antique setting belonged to my mother; look closely at the miniature painting in the living room and you'll see that she's wearing it. Cousin Begoña used to whisper behind her back that a boyfriend of hers ... "

Those ladies in the portraits whom he had seen, had touched, would speak and breathe once more. As I imagined them, I thought I grasped the meaning of the family jewels.

"Have I told you about the time we traveled to Europe in 1908, before the Revolution? First we had to take a boat to Colima ... and in Venice your Aunt Panchita fell in love with these earrings. They were too expensive and I told her so: 'They're fit for a queen.'... The next day I bought them for her. You can't possibly imagine it because you were born long after all this happened, but in those days, in 1908, when we were in Venice, your aunt was so young, so . . . "

"Uncle, you're wearing yourself out; why don't you rest."

"You're right, I am tired. Leave me alone for a while, and take the jewelry box with you to your room; it's yours."

"But Uncle . . . "

"It's all yours, and that's all there is to it! . . . I can give away whatever I feel like."

His voice broke off into a terrible sob: the illusion was vanishing and he once again realized that he was about to die, that he was saying good-bye to his most cherished objects. He turned over in bed and left me standing there holding the box, not knowing what to do.

Other times he would talk to me about the "year of hunger," the "year of the yellow corn," the plague, and he told me ancient tales of murders and apparitions. Once he even tried to sing a *corrido* from his youth but it fell to pieces on his cracked voice. And yet he was passing his life on to me; he was content.

The doctor would say yes, that he did see some improvement, but that we shouldn't get our hopes up, there was no cure. It was only a matter of days.

One afternoon darkened by big, threatening clouds, while I was bringing in the laundry hung in the yard, I heard María's cry. I stood still, listening to that shriek like a thunderbolt, the first of the storm. Then silence, and I was alone in the yard, motionless. A bee buzzed past me and the rain did not start. No one knows as well as I how terrible premonitions are when they're left suspended over a face looking up at the sky.

"Lichita, he's dying! He's at his last gasp!"

"Go get the doctor—No! I'll go . . . call Doña Clara to keep you company while I'm gone."

"And the Father . . . bring the Father."

I ran off, fleeing from that unbearable moment, from that stifled and suffocating imminence. I left, came back, returned to the house, served coffee, received the relatives who were beginning to arrive, already half-dressed in mourning, I sent out for candles, for relics of saints, I kept running madly away in order not to fulfill my one obligation at that moment: to be at my uncle's side. I interrogated the doctor: he had given my uncle a shot for the sake of doing something, but everything was useless by then. Even when I saw the priest arrive with the viaticum, I did not have the strength to go in. I knew I would regret it afterward—*Thank God, now I won't die alone*—but I just couldn't. I covered my face with my hands and began to pray.

The priest came and touched my shoulder. I thought that it was all over and a shiver ran down my spine.

"He's calling for you. Go inside."

I don't know how I got to the threshold. It was nighttime by now and in the candlelight, the room seemed enormous. The furniture had become gigantic, somber, and a strange, stale air hovered over the bed. My skin crawled; my pores exuded horror at all that, at death.

"Go over to him," said the priest.

I obeyed, approaching the foot of the bed, not daring to glance up, not even at the sheets.

"If you have no objections, your uncle would like to marry you *in articulo mortis*, so he can leave you his estate. Do you agree?"

I stifled a cry of horror. I opened my eyes, as if to take in all the terror contained in that room. "Why does he want to drag me with him to the grave?" . . . I felt death rubbing against my own flesh.

"Luisa . . ."

It was Don Apolonio. I had to look at him: he could barely pronounce the syllables; his jaw had gone slack and he talked by moving it like a ventriloquist's dummy.

" . . . please."

And he fell silent, all worn out.

I could bear no more, so I left the room. That was not my uncle; it bore no resemblance to him. He wanted to leave it all to me, yes, not just his estate, but his stories, his life . . . I wanted none of it, neither his life nor his death. None of it. When I opened my eyes I stood in the yard and the sky was still clouded over. I breathed deeply, painfully.

"Is it over?" the relatives came up to ask, when they saw me so upset.

I shook my head no. Behind me the priest spoke.

"Don Apolonio wants to marry her at the last minute, so he can leave her everything."

"And you don't want to?" the elderly maid asked anxiously.

"Don't be silly; you're the one who deserves it. You were like a daughter to them both and you've run yourself ragged taking care of him. If you don't marry him, his nephews in Mexico City aren't going to give you a thing. Don't be silly!"

"How refined of him."

"And afterward you'll be a rich widow, every bit as pure as you are now," a young, lively cousin laughed nervously.

"He has quite a fortune and, as your uncle once removed, I would advise you to . . . "

"If you think it over, refusing to marry him is a denial of charity and humility."

"That's true, that's very true." I didn't want to give the old man that final pleasure, a pleasure that he would be grateful for, after all. My youthful body, with which I was really so pleased, could have no ties with death. I felt sick and that was the last clear thought I had that night. I woke up as from a hypnotic trance when they made me hold his hand bathed in cold sweat. I started to retch again, but I said, "I do."

I remembered vaguely that they had me surrounded the whole time, they were all talking at once, they were leading me here and there, making me sign my name and answer questions. The impression of that night that stayed with me forever was of a malicious group of serenaders spinning giddily around me and laughing grotesquely, chanting

I am the young widow bequeathed by the law

and I, in the middle, was a slave. I was suffering and could not look up at the sky.

When I came to, it was all over, and on my hand there glittered the braided ring I had seen so often on my Aunt Panchita's finger. There had been no time for anything else.

Everyone started to leave.

"If you need me, call me. In the meantime, let him have the drops every six hours."

"May the lord bless you and give you strength."

"Happy wedding night," my young cousin whispered in my ear, with a nasty little laugh.

I returned to the sick man's side. "Nothing has changed, nothing has changed." At least my fear had not changed. I convinced María to stay with me to watch over Don Apolonio, and I only regained control of my nerves when I saw day was breaking. It had begun to rain, but without lightning, without a storm, quietly.

It kept on drizzling all day, and the next day, and even the next. Four days of dying. Our only visitors were the doctor and the priest. On days like that no one leaves home; everyone stays in and waits for life to begin anew. Those are spiritual, nearly sacred days.

If the patient had at least needed lots of attention, the hours would not have seemed so long; but so little could be done for that lethargic body.

On the fourth night, María lay down in a nearby room and left me alone with the dying man. I listened to the monotonous rain and started praying without realizing what I was saying, half asleep and devoid of fear, waiting. My fingers began moving softly, slowly over the rosary beads, and as I caressed them I could feel warmth entering my body through the tips of my fingers, that warmth from another's body that belongs to our own and that we leave, little by little, in objects, only to have it return to us transformed: the companion, the brother who foresees *the other's* sweet warmth, strange and familiar, never felt, inhabiting the marrow of our bones. Softly, deliciously, my nerves calmed, my flesh light, I began to fall asleep.

I must have slept for many hours. It was early morning when I awoke; I could tell because the lights were out, and the electric plant shuts down at two in the morning. The room, dimly lit by the oil lamp burning atop the chest of drawers, at the feet of the Virgin Mary, reminded me of the wedding night, of *my* wedding night . . . That was a long time ago, an empty eternity.

From the depths of the darkness the tired, uneven breathing of Don Apolonio reached me. There he was still, not he, but rather his stubborn, incomprehensible remains that kept lingering on without any purpose, any apparent motive. Death inspires fear, but life mingled with, imbued with death, inspires a horror bearing very little relation to life or death. The silence, decay, stench, monstrous deformation, final extinction: all of it is painful, but it reaches a climax and then begins to recede, begins to dissolve into the earth, into memory, into history. And this did not: the terrible pact between life and death manifesting itself in that useless death rattle might go on forever. I heard him clear his numb throat and it occurred to me that it wasn't air entering that body, or rather it wasn't a human body breathing it in and out; rather, it was a machine panting, then playfully stopping, endlessly killing time. There was no human being there; someone was making child's play out of that snoring. And I was overcome by unspeakable horror: I started breathing to the labored rhythm of the death rattle, to breathe, suddenly stop, suffocate, breathe, suffocate . . . unable to stop, until I realized that I had fooled myself about the meaning of the game, because what I was really feeling was the suffering and asphyxiation of a dying man. Still I kept on, and on, until all that was left was a single breathing, a single inhuman respiration, a single dying process. I felt calmer, terrified but calm: I had knocked down the barrier; I could simply let myself go and wait for our shared death. It seemed to me that through my resignation, my unconditional alliance, *that* would be resolved quickly. It could not go on; it would have achieved its purpose and reached the end of its persistent search in the void.

Not a single good-bye, not a spark of pity for me. I kept on playing that fatal game for a very long time, from a place where time no longer mattered.

Our common breathing became more regular, calmer, but weaker, too. He seemed to come back. But I was so tired that I could not move; I could feel the lethargy coming to rest permanently in my body. I opened my eyes. Nothing had changed.

No. Far away, in the shadows, there is a rose, a single rose, unique and alive. There it is, clear as can be, with its large, airy petals, radiant. It is a beautiful and simple presence. I look at it and my hand moves and recalls its touch and the simple action of placing it in the vase. I looked at it then; I recognize it now. I move slightly, blink, and it is still there, complete, identical to itself.

I breathe freely, with my own respiration. I pray, remember, doze off, and the pure rose stands guard over light and secrets.

Death and hope are transformed.

But now day begins to break and in the clear sky I see (at last!) that the rainy days are over. I sit gazing out the window for a long time, at how everything changes when the sun rises. A powerful ray of light comes in and the dying strikes me as a lie; an unwarranted joy fills my lungs and I inadvertently smile. I turn to the rose as to an accomplice, but I do not find it; the sun has withered it. The luminous days, the enervating heat, returned; people would work, sing, but Don Apolonio did not die; rather, he seemed to be getting better. I kept on taking care of him, but glumly now, with my eyes downcast, unburdening myself of all my guilty and exacerbated self-denial in the pains I took to wait on him. What I wanted, with absolute clarity now, was for it all to end soon, for him finally to die. The fear, the horror that the sight of him, his touch, his voice, inspired in me was unjustified, because the bond uniting us was not real, it could not be; and yet I felt it weighing on me, and by dint of kindness and remorse I hoped to free myself from it.

Yes, Don Apolonio was getting better before our very eyes. Even the doctor was surprised; he could not explain it.

It was precisely the morning when I propped him up on cushions for the first time that I caught that glimmer in my uncle's eyes. The heat was stifling and I had had nearly to lift him up in the air. When I set him down, I noticed it: the old man was staring fixedly at my heaving chest, his face distorted and his trembling hands unconsciously reaching out to me. I instinctively drew back, turning my head away.

"Close the shutters, please, it's too hot."

His half-dead body was getting excited.

"Come here, Luisa. Sit next to me. Come here."

"Yes, Uncle." I sat down, timidly, at the foot of the bed, without looking up at him.

"Don't call me Uncle, call me Polo; after all, now we're more intimately related." There was a hint of mockery in his tone of voice.

"Yes, Uncle."

"Polo, Polo." His voice was once again sweet and smooth. "You'll have to forgive me for a lot of things. I'm old and sick, and a man in that condition is like a child."

"Yes."

"Let's see. Say, 'Yes, Polo.'"

"Yes, Polo."

On my lips that name sounded like an aberration; it made me feel an unsurmountable loathing.

And Polo got better, but he became cranky and fussy. I realized he was struggling to go back to the way he had been; but no, the man resuscitating was not him, but someone else.

"Luisa, bring me . . . Luisa, give me . . . Luisa, fluff my pillows . . . bring me some water . . . straighten my leg."

He wanted me around him all day long, coming close to him, touching him. And that fixed gaze and that distorted face I had seen that first day reappeared more and more often. They began to superimpose themselves on his features, like a mask.

"Pick up my book. It fell under the bed, on this side."

I got down on my knees and stuck my head and most of my torso under the bed, but I had to stretch my arm out as far as I could in order to reach it. At first I thought it had been my own movement, or perhaps the bedclothes brushing up against me, but when I had retrieved the book and was starting to get up, I suddenly froze, dumbfounded by what I had foreseen, expected: the release, the cry, the thunderbolt. A rage I had never felt shook me, once I managed to convince myself that what was happening was real, and that, taking advantage of my shock, his trembling hand was becoming steadier and firmer, and was amusing itself; emboldened, unchecked, it was groping, exploring my hips, a cadaverous hand sticking to my flesh and squeezing it with delight, a dead hand impatiently seeking the cavity between my legs, an autonomous, a disembodied hand.

I got up as quickly as I could, my face burning with anger and shame, but once I faced him I forgot myself and walked like a robot into the nightmare: he was laughing softly, with his toothless mouth. And then, suddenly serious, with a coldness that terrified me:

"Well! Aren't you my wife before God and mankind? Come here; I'm cold; warm up my bed. But take off your dress; you're going to crumple it."

Now I know that what followed is my story, my life, but I can barely remember it, like a repulsive dream; I don't even know if it lasted a very short time or a very long one. There was one idea that kept me going at first: "This can't go on; it can't go on." I believed God would not permit it, that He would prevent it somehow. He, personally. Once so fearful, death now seemed my only salvation. Not Apolonio's salvation, no, he was a demon of death; but mine, the just and necessary death for my rotten flesh. But nothing happened. Everything went on, suspended in time, with no possible future. Then one morning, without packing a suitcase, I left.

It was useless. Three days later they notified me that my husband was dying and was calling for me. I went to see the confessor and told him my story.

"What keeps him going is lust, the most horrible of sins. That's no life, Father, it's death. Let him die!"

"He would die in despair. We can't allow that."

"And what about me?"

"I understand, but if you don't go back it will be murder. Try not to excite him; put your trust in the Virgin, and think about your duty . . . "

I returned. And sin pulled him out of the grave again.

Struggling, endlessly struggling, with the passing of the years I was finally able to overcome, to overcome my hatred, and in the end, the very end, I also managed to tame the beast: Apolonio died at peace, sweetly, himself again.

But I could never go back to being the person I was. Now villainy and evil gleam in the eyes of the men who look at me and I feel like the cause of everyone's sin, worse than the lowliest of prostitutes. All alone, a sinner, totally consumed by the implacable flame enveloping all of us who, like ants, inhabit this cruel summer that never ends.

Mariana

Mariana used to wear a navy-blue uniform and she had the desk next to mine. In the row in front of us was Concha Zazueta. Mariana didn't pay any attention to the lesson; she would amuse herself drawing little houses with sloping roofs and trees and cloud figures, and a road leading up to the house, and ducks and chickens, the sort of thing that first graders draw. We were in the sixth grade. It's hot, the afternoon sun is coming in through the windows; the Rev. Mother Paz, standing in front of the blackboard, takes forever to explain the Peloponnesian War. She tells us about the Greek aristocracy's hatred of the imposing Athenian democracy. Funny. From my point of view, the only true aristocracy was precisely the Athenians', and Pericles was the image that lent that aristocracy its power; it seems to me that even the plague over Athens, which targeted "the most select segment of the population," underscored that reality. All of this is more of a feeling than a thought. Although she doesn't say so, Mother Paz, too, is on the Athenians' side. It's lovely to watch her explain—reconstructing in the air, with her delicate hands, the buildings she has never seen—the splendor of the condemned city. Mother Paz feels a loving need to save Athens, but she also feels the peculiar pleasure of knowing that the perfect city would perish, seemingly without grandeur, sadly; apparently, in history, but not in truth. Mariana nudges me. "See? Here's the little road that Fernando walks down and here's me standing in the doorway, waiting for him," and she very proudly points out two little dolls, one wearing a hat and the other one with hair just like the clouds and trees, stiff and awkward, in the middle of the stupid drawing. "They're very ugly," I tell her, so she'll leave me alone, and she responds, "I'm going to make them over again." She turns the page in her notebook and meticulously sets about drawing a scene identical to the previous one. Pericles has died by now, but I'm sure Mariana has never heard of him.

I never went with her; Concha Zazueta was the one who would tell me all about it.

After school was out, we would sit under the palm tree and eat the tart dates fallen on the lawn, while Concha would fill me in, little by little, on where they had gone in the car that Fernando would steal from his father while it was parked in front of the bank. In the cotton fields, the orchards, next to Black Bridge, everywhere, it seemed, was bursting with marvelous places for them to run off to, to kiss and roll around in each other's arms, dying of laughter. Neither Concha nor I had suspected that something very like paradise on earth was growing around us. Concha would say, " . . . and he sat there looking at her, gazing right into her eyes, dead serious, as if he were angry or very sad, and she laughed silently and threw back her head and he drew closer, closer, and he looked at her. He seemed sort of desperate, but all at once he closed his eyes and kissed her; I didn't think he was ever going to let go of her. When he opened his eyes, the sunlight hurt them. Then he caressed one of her hands, as if he were ashamed . . . I had a perfect view of it all, because I was in the backseat, and they didn't even notice."

Oh my God! Those stories really made Concha feel important; and she made us practically beg her to tell them, even though she loved doing it and blushing and seeing how the rest of us would blush.

"Why did Mariana laugh if Fernando was so serious?"

"Who knows. Have you ever been kissed?"

"No."

"Me either."

So we couldn't understand those changes or what they meant.

More and more episodes, details, lots of details, started piling up inside us from Concha Zazueta's stories: Fernando would tug, a little at a time, through a tiny hole, at the red bow on Mariana's uniform, while telling her about something that had happened at a meeting of the university federation; he would pull a little at a time, without meaning to, but when the knot finally unraveled and the ribbon flopped down onto Mariana's chest, they would both burst out laughing, and holding each other, shaking with laughter, they would forget all about the federation. There were also fights over inexplicable things, over meaningless words, over nothing, but most of all they would kiss and he would call her lovely. I never heard him say it, but even now I feel breathless when I remember the way he would say it, all choked up, pressing her against him, while Concha Zazueta held her breath in a corner of the backseat.

It was the following year, when we were already in the first year of the business program, that Mariana arrived at school one day with her lips scarlet red. Mother Julia was livid when she saw her.

"Go to the bathroom at once and take that filth off your face. Then straight to Mother Superior's office."

Mariana walked slowly toward the restroom. She returned with her lips blotted dry and tinged a very discreet red.

"Didn't I tell you to take *all* that horrible paint off your face?"

"Yes, Mother, but since it's very good lipstick, the kind my mother wears, it won't come off."

She said it in her slow, affected voice, as if she were teaching a lesson to a child. Mother Julia turned pale with rage.

"You won't be eligible for any prizes this year. You hear me?"

"Yes, Mother."

"You're going to go to the Mother Superior's office . . . I'm going to call your parents. . . . And you're going to write a thousand times, "I shall be obliging toward my superiors, and . . . and . . . understood?"

"Yes, Mother."

Mother Julia went on to invent a few more punishments, but they didn't worry Mariana in the least.

"Why did you come to school wearing makeup?"

"It would have been worse for people to see this. Look."

And she bit her lower lip so we could see the bottom side: it was split into little grooves and the skin was broken, although it was covered up with lipstick.

"What happened?"

"Fernando."

"What did Fernando do to you?"

She smiled and shrugged, gazing at us with pity.

One morning, before the bell rang to go to class, Concha came up to me, all worked up, and said:

"Last night her dad hit her. I was there because they invited me to supper. Her dad yelled and Mariana said she wouldn't give Fernando up for anything in the world. Then Don Manuel hit her. He hit her in the face about three times. He was so furious that we were all scared, but not Mariana. She sat there quietly, looking at him. Blood was running out of the corner of her mouth, but she didn't cry or say a single word. Don Manuel shook her by the shoulders, but she just stood there, looking at him. Then he let go of her and left. Mariana wiped her mouth and looked at her blood-stained hand. Her mom was crying. 'I'm going to bed,' Mariana told me, absolutely calm, and went into her room. I was trembling. I left without even saying good-night; I went home and could barely sleep. I'm not going to hang around with her anymore: I'm afraid her dad will get like that again. I'm sure she's not coming today."

But when the bell rang, Mariana came in with her leisurely walk and her head held high, just like every morning. Her lower lip was swollen and there was a cut on the left side, near the corner of her mouth, but she was perfectly groomed and serene.

"What happened?" Lilia Chávez asked her.

"I fell down," she answered, looking slyly at Concha. "Piss

ant," she murmured into Concha's ear as she went by, on her way to sit with the older kids.

Piss Ant was what we called Piss Ant Zazueta for years afterward. Beatings, boarding school, punishments, trips, they tried everything to make Mariana give up Fernando, and she accepted the pain of the beatings and the pleasure of traveling, without compromising herself. We knew that there was an empty time that her parents could fill however they wanted, but that afterward Fernando's time would come. And that's what happened. When Mariana came home from boarding school, they ran away together, then they came home, asked to be forgiven, and their parents made them get married. It was a lavish wedding that we all attended. I've never seen two such beautiful creatures: radiant, free at last.

Of course, the white dress and the orange blossoms created a scandal, people talking a lot about the elopement, but underneath it all everything was so normal that I thought how absurd Don Manuel was for not letting them get engaged in the first place. Even though she would have been thirteen or fourteen then, if he hadn't opposed it with that inexplicable ferocity. . . . But no, there lying on top of the table were Fernando's hand and Mariana's hand, his fingers on top of hers, without caresses, forgotten; you could see at a glance the presence of that resting contact, until it was practically a glow or a weight, something more than two hands touching. There was no father or reason capable of obliterating the giddy, inexpressible and certain reality of those two hands, distinct and yet together.

He is gloomy at his daughter's wedding, because she's marrying a good boy, the son of family friends—and he greets the well-wishers with a smile, but deep down in his eyes there is a bitter void. It isn't anger or spite, it's a void. Mariana goes past him, dancing with Fernando. Mariana. On her luminous face I suddenly see the split lip, the pallid skin, and I realize that on that day, on our way into class, her face was closed. Serene and sure of herself, walking steadily, defiant, she bears the wound, the pallor, the silence; she closes herself and keeps walking, without allowing herself to doubt, or to confide in anyone, or to cry. Her mouth swells up more and more and in her eyes is the stifled pain, the pain that I didn't see then or at any other time, the pain that I recognize but have never felt: a slow, dark, silent trickle that gradually fills up, floods the eyes until they explode into a final flash of fear. But there is no fear, there are no screams, there is the void necessary for pain to begin to fill it. I blink and realize that Mariana isn't there, she's already gone by, and the split lip, the paler and paler face, and the eyes, especially the eyes, belong to her father.

I didn't want to see Mariana's dead body, but I saw Don Manuel during the wake and recognized Mariana's decomposed face in his distorted features: once again, that terrible mixture of future and past, of pure suffering, impersonal yet embodied in a person, in two people, one alive and the other dead, both of them blind now and drowned in the dark current that they surrendered themselves to, for their own sake and for the sake of others, many others, or for the sake of someone else.

Mariana was here, on that velvet sofa, the color of gold, sitting with her legs crossed, hunched over, holding a wineglass. Around her, the velvet ripples. I remember her yellow eyes, docile and waiting. "The victim was thirty-four years old." You never thought about age when you looked at Mariana. I came here to evoke her— Mariana, inside your house and along with you. Wait: she would drag sluggish syllables and words out for whole minutes, silly words that she let out slowly, arching her mouth, words that meant nothing to her and that she gradually let go of, savoring them, taking advantage of them in order to relish the sound of her own voice. A false voice, I know, but the one she sought and found, the only voice that was truly hers. It created a mood, a sort of mood, in herself, in you, in me, in the mood itself, but there was something else . . . do you remember? She loved to say awful things in that hoarse voice of hers, and then turn her head, pretending to be bored, stroking her neck with one hand, while the rest of us would die of laughter. The pearls, that long string of pearls that she would hide behind, smiling, nibbling at it, showing herself off. The gestures, the movements. Vamping it up, or pretending to be carefree, or playing the role of the dancer or the sensual woman. Saying who she was that way, while she would sing, drink, dance. But she didn't tell us everything. . . . Do you realize that we never saw her kiss Fernando? And we've seen others do it, even married people having an affair, early one morning, but not them; they would go off and make out in secret. She died in secret, although the scandal has spread like a stain, although they displayed her nakedness, her most private self, what they thought was her most private self. Mariana's slow and frenetic time was inside of her, deep inside, it didn't go away. A blind groping, that had nothing to do with intelligence. I know you think I'm doing the wrong thing, that this rage over someone else's story is unnatural. But it isn't someone else's. It has also happened for your sake and for mine. . . . Madness and crime . . . Did you ever think that the stories that end the way they should stand apart from the rest, exist in an absolute way? In a time that doesn't go away.

Poking around, I ended up at the jail. I went to see the murderer.

He's innocent. No, I mean, he's guilty, he has committed murder. But he doesn't know it.

When I went in he looked at me in a way that made me aware of my appearance, my manners: elegant. The farthest thing from my mind was that I would feel elegant in a jail cell, standing before a murderer.

Yes, he killed her, with those hands that, terrified, he shows off, shocked by them.

He doesn't know why, he doesn't know why, and he bursts into tears. He didn't know her. A friend, another traveler, had spoken to him about her—and everything went exactly as his friend had told him, except the end, when the pleasure was drawn out for a long time, a very long time, and he realized that pleasure consisted of strangling her. Why didn't she defend herself? If she had screamed, or had scratched him, it wouldn't have happened, but she didn't seem to be suffering. The worst part was that she was looking at him. But he didn't realize he was killing her. He didn't want to, he had no reason to kill her. He knows that he killed her, but he doesn't believe it. He can't believe it. And he is wracked with sobs. He begs my forgiveness, he gets down on his knees. He talks to me about his parents, down in Sayula. He has always been good, I can ask anyone in his town. I say that I know, because that's how the rewards of innocence often are. My words sound strange to him, and he keeps on crying. I feel sorry for him. When I leave the cell, he is stretched out on the floor, face down, crying. He is a victim.

I went off to Mexico City to see Fernando. He wasn't surprised I would make such a long trip in order to talk to him. My explanations seemed natural. If what he told me had been a little less true, he might have even been grateful to have me as a witness. But he and Mariana don't need witnesses; they're each other's witnesses. Fernando doesn't hesitate to open himself up. Mariana's bottomless time triumphs inside him, or was it he who gave it to her? In any case, Fernando's story gives meaning to the unconnected, deranged facts that, in our minds, constitute the truth of the story. In his confession, I found what I had been looking for: the secret that makes Mariana's story absolute.

"On the day of the wedding she was incredibly beautiful. Her eyes had an animal-like purity, prior to all sin. At the instant she received the blessing, I sensed the chill of pleasure running up and down her body. The contact with 'something' beyond the senses made her tremble violently, not in her major nerves, but in the little, secondary nerves that cover the skin; I stroked her back gently, and felt how they vibrated again; I could almost see her naked back shaking a section at a time, blemish by blemish, with a feline movement. Now things were looking up: Mariana was consecrated . . . to me. But I was fooling myself: her eyes were wide open, gazing at the altar. Only I saw that fixed gaze absorbing a mystery that no one could put into words. When she turned toward me they were still filled with emptiness.

"I should have felt fear or respect, but no, a strange frenzy, an insatiable need for possession, blinded me, and that was the beginning of what they call my madness.

"You might say that that madness gave birth to our four children; but that isn't so; love, the flesh, existed too, and for years they were enough to pacify the spiritual passion that shone for the first time that day. We were granted many years of passionate and honorable happiness. That's why I believe, right now, that we're engulfed by a great wave of mercy.

"It was another moment of immense happiness that marked us forever.

"The sun was weightless; a cold, steady wind blew over the deserted marshes; beyond the sand dunes you could hear the sea; there were only scrubby mangroves and sands filled with nitrate, smooth, hard, impenetrable roads, strangely like the pale, still sky. Footsteps don't leave a trace in the marshes, all the paths look alike, and yet you never tire of the marshes, you walk them forever surprised at their naked, inhospitable beauty. Holding hands, we reached the edge of Dautillos Swamp.

"It was she who showed me her eyes, innocently, shamelessly. Once again there was no gaze; they were bottomless, incapable of serving as mirrors, totally emptied of me. Then she turned to the sand dunes and stood there quietly.

"The rage that I felt on our wedding day, the terrible jealousy that something, someone could bring out that icy gaze in Mariana, my carnal, silly Mariana; jealousy of a soul that existed naturally and that was not for me; jealousy of that slow absorption at the altar, in beauty, of some nourishment that she needed, that must make its demands on her, always crouching inside of her, and wanting nothing to do with me. Immense fury and jealousy that made me beat her, carry her into the water, strangle her, drown her, forever seeking the gaze that wasn't mine. But Mariana's eyes, open, constantly open, reflected only me; with surprise, fear, love, pity. That's what I remember above all, her eyes under the water, bulging out of their sockets, looking at me with immense pity. Since then I have remembered the wet hair stuck to her neck, which seemed infantile at the time; the blood running out of her mouth, out of her ear; the hoarse scream of her death and my masculine love crying out alongside her voice, the dreadful pain of seeing her wounded, suffering, half dead, while my soul kept on murdering her in order to at last elicit her unfathomable gaze, in order to touch her at that final moment, when she would no longer be able to look at me, and would have no choice but to look at me as at her own death. I wanted to be her death.

"And yes, there was an instant when her empty eyes, fixed on mine, filled me with that unknown thing, beyond her and me, an abyss that I didn't know how to look into, where I was lost as if in a terrible night. I let go of her, dragged her body to the bank and screamed, screamed, lying across her stomach, while I watched the countless little holes, the bubbles, the blind movements, the swarming horror, calm and pitiless, of the swamp's inhabitants; vile manifestations of life, neither worms nor tadpoles, disgusting, formless, awkward, minuscule, living, silent creatures that made me cry over my enormous sin, and understand it, and love it.

"Since then I've been here. I take the pills and pretend I've forgotten. I behave myself, I'm friendly, concur with all the good explanations that the doctor gives me and willingly admit I'm mad. But they don't realize how much harm they're doing me. The first thing I remember after it was all over was someone telling me Mariana was still alive; then I wanted to go to her, beg her forgiveness, I cried in pain and remorse, I wrote to her, but they wouldn't let us near each other. I know she came here, she begged them, but they were also looking out for her well-being and they didn't let her in. They said that ours was a destructive passion, not seeing that the only thing that could save us was desire, love, flesh, which offered us tenderness and respite.

"Their treatments succeeded in depriving me of everything that was good for me: sex, strength, the happiness of a healthy animal, and they left me alone with what I think to myself and will never tell them.

"As for her, they abandoned her to her unrequited passion. Then they acted surprised when she started openly going off to hotels, with the first guy she met. Once, when I said that she was doing it to be faithful to us, that they had left her no other way to search for me, they were so alarmed that they wanted to operate on me immediately. For my own good and the sake of my health they'll castrate me in every way possible, until nothing is left but innocent and enviable, primitive, true life: the life of the creatures that live at the edges of swamps.

"I'm grateful I can say what I have to, before they force me to forget it or not understand it: I killed Mariana. It was I, using the hands of that wretch Anselmo Pineda, the traveling salesman; it was I that Mariana was searching for in other men's bodies: no one ever touched her but me; I was her death—she gazed into my eyes and that's why I feel nothing but contempt for what they're going to do to me, but I'm not afraid, because there's something much more dreadful than the idiocy awaiting me: Mariana's final gaze in the hotel room, as she was strangled, that gaze encompassing all of silence, impossibility, eternity, the place where we no longer exist, where I will never find her again."

The Sign

The dense, immobile sun imposed its presence; reality was paralyzed under its implacable cruelty. In the atmosphere, there floated the omen of a suspended, burning death, without putrefaction but also without tenderness. It was three in the afternoon.

Pedro, weighed down, nearly defeated, walked under the sun. The deserted streets lost their meaning in the dazzling light. The heat, dry and dreadful like an execution without a hangman, cut his breath short. But it didn't matter: inside himself he always found a sharp, icy, mortifying place that was worse than the sun, but was also a refuge, a sort of revenge, against it.

He reached the little plaza and sat down under the great laurel-of-India tree. Silence formed a cavity around thought. He had to stretch his legs, move his arm, in order to avoid perpetuating the stillness of the plants and of the air within himself. He got up and, walking around the tree, stood looking at the cathedral.

It had always been there, but only now did he

see that it existed in another climate, a cool climate that understood its absent look of a dreamy adolescent. The adolescent quality wasn't hard to detect; it had to do with the rumpled grace of its proportions: too tall and thin. Pedro had known the humble history of this defect since he was a child: It was originally intended to have three naves, but there had been barely enough money to finish the largest one; and that initial poverty was faithfully reproduced in its clean lines, like those of a mountain chapel—which is why it evoked pine trees. He crossed the street and went in, without thinking that he was entering a church.

There was no one inside, only the sexton stirring like a shadow in the semidarkness of the presbytery. Not a noise was to be heard. He sat down halfway up the aisle, gazing at the altars, the paper flowers . . . he thought about the distracted prayer that someone else might say, the person who usually sat in that pew, and for an instant he almost wished he could believe like that, deep down, unenthusiastically, but just enough to get by.

The soft, yellow sun came in through the tall stained-glass windows, and the atmosphere was cool. You could sit there without thinking, take a break from yourself, from despair and hope. And he grew calm, empty, enveloped in the coolness and watching the attenuated sun slip in through the stained-glass windows.

Then he heard the footsteps of someone walking in timidly, furtively. He wasn't concerned; he didn't even shift his position, but remained lost in that indifferent sense of well-being, until the person who had come in was standing beside him and spoke to him.

At first he thought he hadn't understood and he turned to look at the man. His face was so close that he could even make out the sweaty pores, the wrinkles alongside the tired mouth. It was a worker. His face, the face that it would later occur to him he had seen more closely than any other, was a face like thousands, millions: broad, weatherbeaten. But he also saw the gray eyes and the nearly transparent eyelids with their stubby eyelashes, and the gaze, that inexpressive, naked gaze.

"Will you let me kiss your feet?"

He repeated it, relentless. His voice was somewhat tense, but he held it steady; he had fully assumed his role and expected the other man to be equal to it, without any need for explanations. It wasn't right, there was no reason to involve him, it wasn't possible! It was all so unexpected, so absurd. . . . But the sun was there, still and sweet, and the sexton began calmly lighting some candles. Pedro mumbled an apology for not being able to comply. The man turned to look at him. His eyes could make one do anything, but they were only asking.

"Pardon me, sir. It's hard for me, too, but I have to do it."

He had to. And if Pedro didn't help him, who would? Who was going to swallow the inhuman humiliation of having another person kiss one's feet? What a meager dose of charity and purity fit into a man's soul. Pedro took pity on him.

"All right."

"Would you mind taking off your shoes?"

It was too much. The blood was pounding in his ears, he was beside himself, but lucid, so lucid that he foresaw his disgust at the contact, his shame at his nakedness, and afterward his remorse and multiple torment without beginning or end. He knew this, but he took his shoes off anyway.

Being barefoot like that, like him, defenseless and humbled, consenting to be the source of another person's humiliation . . . no one would ever know what it was like . . . like dying in disgrace, something eternally cruel.

He didn't look at the worker, but he felt his disgust, disgust at his feet and at him, at all men. And even so, he had kneeled down with such great respect that it made him think that at that moment, for that human being, he had ceased being a man and was the image of something more sacred.

A shiver ran through him and he closed his eyes. . . . But the hot lips touched him, stuck to his skin . . . it was love, a love expressed from flesh to flesh, from man to man, but that maybe. . . . Disgust was there, disgust at them both. Because in the first instant, as the man's hot mouth barely brushed him, he had thought it an aberration. He had gone so far as that, so he would later feel more tormented . . . no, no, both of them felt disgusted, except that in addition to that there was love. It had to be said, you had to dare think once, just once, about the Crucifixion.

The man stood up and said, "Thank-you"; he looked at Pedro with his cleansed eyes, and left.

Pedro stayed there, alone with his bare feet, so very much his and yet so alien now. Feet with a stigmata.

This sign is inside me forever; I don't know whether it is the sign of this world and its sin or the sign of a desolate redemption.

Why me? His feet looked so innocent, they were just like everyone else's feet, but they had open wounds and only he knew it. He had to look at them, had to put on his socks, his shoes . . . now it seemed to him that his greatest shame consisted of that, of not being able to go barefoot, without hiding, to be faithful. *I don't deserve it; I'm not worthy.* He was crying.

When he left the church the sun had already gone down. He would never remember completely all he had thought and suffered at the time. All he knew was that he had to accept that a man had kissed his feet and that it had changed everything; that it was, forever more, the most important and intimate thing in his life, but that he would never know, in any sense, what it meant.

New Year's Eve

For Vita

I was alone. When we passed by a subway station in Paris, I noticed that it was striking midnight. I was very unhappy, for other reasons. The tears began to fall, silently.

He looked at me. A black man. We were both hanging from straps, face to face. He watched me tenderly, wanting to console me. Strangers, never exchanging a word. The gaze is the most profound thing that exists. He kept his eyes fixed on mine until the tears dried. At the next station he got off.

Underground River

For Huberto Batis

I have led a solitary life for many years, a woman alone in this immense house, a cruel and exquisite life. That's the story I want to tell: about the cruelty and exquisiteness of a rural life. I am going to speak about the other, about what is usually kept to oneself, about what one thinks and what one feels when one doesn't think. I want to tell everything that has built up over time in a provincial soul that polishes it, caresses and perfects it without anyone suspecting. You might think I'm too ignorant to try to explain this story that you already know, but I'm sure you don't know it well. You don't take into account the river and its avenues, the tolling of the bells, or the screams. You haven't forever been trying to figure out the meaning of the inexplicable things, together in the world, the terrible things, the sweet things. You haven't had to give up what is called a normal life in order to follow the path of what you don't understand, in order to be faithful to it. You didn't struggle day and night to clarify a few words: to have a destiny. I have a destiny, but it isn't mine. I have to live my life according to other people's destinies. I am the guardian of the forbidden, of what can't be explained, of what inspires shame, and I have to stay here and watch over it, so it can't get out, but also so it will exist. So it will exist and the balance will be struck. So it won't get out to harm other people.

This is what I learned from Sofía, who learned it from Sergio, who had in turn posed it to himself when he saw his brother Pablo, your father, go mad.

I feel it has been my lot to live beyond rupture, beyond limits, on the other side, where everything I do seems to be, but isn't, an attack on nature. If I stopped I would be committing a crime. I have always been tempted to run away. Sofía wasn't; Sofía even seemed proud, since she was able to build toward madness. I manage only to keep it alive.

So that you won't have to come see it for yourself, I'll try to explain to you what Sofía did with this house, which used to be just like any other. It's easy to identify because it's isolated; it has no continuity with the rest: on one side it borders on the large, vacant lot where Sergio didn't build, and on the other the black ruins of your father's house. Aside from that, it has a facade like all the others: an entranceway with three barred windows on the right and three on the left. But inside it is different.

It's a house like many others, with three hallways in the shape of a U, but in the middle, instead of a courtyard, this house has a splendid staircase, with steps as wide as the entrance door with its five Gothic arches. It descends slowly, step by step, opens onto a platform, then keeps going down until it reaches what was once the river's edge, when the river was high. You can't imagine how beautiful it is.

Level with the platform, four rooms were dug out, two on either side of the staircase, so they were situated below the side hallways, and they seem to have been there always, to have held up the upper part of the house. Maybe it's true. These four rooms are richly hand carved; Sofía thought that, since her father couldn't have any comforts, not even furniture, he should enjoy some sort of extraordinary luxury. There are four rooms, but only one of them has really been used, the first one on the left, as you go down to the river. I haven't been able to stop thinking about Sofía's motives for having four rooms built, one for each of us, or whether the proportions of the staircase and platform that they rest on simply required that number.

In one of them was your father, when Sergio and Sofía decided that they should build a place for him here, a place that was uniquely his in the world. Neither of them left here to bring him home, but afterward they took great pains to take care of him. They listened attentively to all his inhuman shrieks; they built their lives around them.

It was no one's fault that he escaped from the hard-carved room. Maybe you think that someone left the door unlocked or left the key within reach of his hand, but if ever you had seen the river come when it has risen, ever heard how its earthly din, like an earthquake, fills the air before you see the first, terrible wave sweeping away houses, cattle, the dead, you would know he had to leave the room like the river leaves its bed, to destroy things and destroy himself, so that another life, different and the same, perhaps your life, could begin again.

If you understood this you would know that his setting a house on fire, the house he had inherited, was no accident, nor was it an accident that he died in its flames. You, for example, can have someone else sell that vacant lot for you, but if you thought there was a house here in your name, you would have to come here. That's why this other house where we now live won't be left to you; I saw to that. But Sergio's lot does belong to you, because you don't have to see it.

I don't want to tell you about your father's death, nor about Sergio's death; I only hope you'll learn to see them differently, and that's why I'm telling you this other story, about the life we had.

You could feel, by the light of the oil lamp, beneath the pale skin of their restless mouths, in the stony silence of the hands lying in their laps, the dull hum of struggle filling the silence of the room, of the house, of the night. They were my brothers and sister, but I didn't understand yet. Rather, they were brothers and sister, each other's brothers and sister. There was no physical resemblance between them, aside from their slender bodies and their skin that grew transparent around the eyelids. Yet they turned what seemed like difference into agreement: the rhythm to which they moved, their hands, their deep, ecstatic eyes, like pools, lent them a powerful resemblance that went beyond facial features and coloring. Their ages and education were also different, but no one would have believed it.

That voluntary resemblance was a defense that they erected. But I've already said that I'll tell you only what is strictly necessary about that struggle. The truth is that it all began before I could understand it, and I'll transmit it to you as my memory, not time or reason, dictates.

The night of the looting transpired differently for us than for other people: We stood side by side in the window, looking out, and our front hall was the only one that no one attacked, because as soon as he heard the shouts coming up the road from the Bebelama, Sergio walked slowly out, opened it up, turned on the lights all through the house, checked his tie in the hall mirror, and sat down to wait, his back absentmindedly resting against the window frame; Sofía went over and sat down on the stone bench, and they didn't exchange a word.

I saw them come into the plaza; on foot, on horseback, shouting and shooting and breaking down doors, laughing loudly, for no reason, and I was afraid. I went up to Sofía, took her hand, and she smiled and sat me down next to her; then she turned away so she could keep watching.

Pushing and shoving, they dragged the priest out through the archways of the sacristy. It pained me to see his pale, contorted face move from light to darkness, from a laugh to a blow, to a curse, stumbling over the plants, making the canaries shriek. If you saw it now, in the morning, that same sacristy with its arches, you couldn't imagine what it was like. You can only gauge the size of a man's shadow when he's standing before the flames.

"They only want money. But he likes the idea of becoming a martyr. I detest martyrs," said Sergio. I felt his disdain toward that pale, familiar face that we had seen day in and day out since we were born, and that was suffering. I shuddered violently; Sofía squeezed my fingers firmly and placed her other hand on my shoulder.

When they came into our house, I was afraid they would detect the nearly ironic curiosity in Sergio's eyes, and there was one man who stopped in front of him and was about to say something. Whether or not Sergio smiled or altered his expression, I don't know, but he kept right on watching the other man with those eyes with the golden speck in the middle, and the other guy went off and slashed up a sofa. It's still here, discolored and with the stuffing hanging out, and it's very calming to look at, I don't know why; maybe because it doesn't shout and it has remained the same for thirty years.

When I think about it now, it seems to me that we must have looked like a family portrait, the three of us standing in the window frame, but at that moment it was the first time I felt that we, including myself, were separate, and that they couldn't touch us.

From the other side of the square, Rosalía was shrieking and a man was chasing her. Over the gunfire, you could hear the shrill screams of women.

Actually, they left our house very quickly, since nothing was under lock and key. Sergio must have done that several days earlier without our noticing, or maybe as he turned on all the lights, as if we were giving a big party. They left hurriedly, without speaking to us, and little by little a trail of what they had taken was left, abandoned in bars and on the streets, but we never made any attempt to get it back; we understood that it was no longer ours.

"I thought it would be different," said Sergio, when silence began to fall and a leaden light in the sky made me queasy. As he walked by, he caressed the oil lamp. "I'm glad no one noticed how beautiful its pink light is," he said.

He shut the door and we went to bed.

During the following nights, when the patrols would go by and you could hear "Who goes there?" and stray gunfire and the dogs, Sergio explained the festivals of the different gods to Sofía. "Sacred disorder," I remember his saying, and things like that. I could quote you more phrases, but the phrases don't matter. It's strange that what mattered to him about that night wasn't the business of the priest, or Rosalía, or the hanged people, it was that those men's merriment was false, that they were wrong; instead of those hollow horselaughs, they should have screamed, shrieked, killed, and robbed, with truth, with sorrow, "because as it was it was just like a party." And the truth was that he felt sorry for those men.

We didn't learn about revolutions from that revolution,

but rather, about cults, rites, and ancient gods. That's the way he taught us so many things: so we would understand other things, not similar ones, but ones that might explain them.

He could tell you, for example, that your mother was your mother because she had given birth to you, but that a true mother is one that *chooses* you afterward, not because you're a child, but because you're the way you are; that's why it seemed natural to him that a queen should hate or disdain her son from a very early age. One of the things we read about was the history of France; I remember it perfectly.

The truth is that Sofía and I would study whatever was offered to us—as a topic or as an example—and he would talk to us about it at night, without any plan, with no rhyme or reason. He wasn't a professor, nor did he like to hear himself talk; he would stumble along, reframing his arguments. As I said, he would follow the trail out loud, sometimes in our presence. But on the nights when he was silent and gloomy, what was he looking for?

By the light of the oil lamp I first heard about you, about Pablo, your father, who gradually became so young that I could barely remember him. You were a baby and your father was already in a sanitarium. He never saw you. Don't draw closer to him now. Remember, he's only a dead man.

I also heard about the staircase. The flame didn't flicker; it held still, and its tenuous clarity cast warm tones on my siblings' pale flesh. Sofía would sew or embroider, while Sergio held a book in his hands; sometimes he would read a little. I heard them talk quietly about you and your father, about madness, as if it were all memories. Sofía would get the mail in the morning, but she would wait until night to tell us softly, as if it were an old story, that Pablo had strange mental disorders or that it had become necessary to send him to an insane asylum.

Pablo was always lively, spirited; he liked to sing, pick our mother up and swing her around, and let her scream while he laughed. Spirited and strong, very strong. Or maybe we saw him that way because he was much older. But they say that now he has become violent, that there are times when he destroys everything he can get his hands on, and when he wants to kill. Strength and happiness combined, together with an exasperation that corrupts and spoils happiness, can turn into violence; or is it anger alone that takes control of a man and bleeds away all his vitality? Where does that anger come from and where does it spread to—where does it lurk? It falls over him like a bolt of lightning, possesses him like a demon, and he is only being himself, and it's necessary to lock him up in a safe place, in an asylum, where there are people who are acquainted with that urge to destroy and aren't afraid of it.

That's how she would tell the news. Sergio would keep silent and she would go on talking; he would question her sweetly until he himself started talking about madness, about the staircase, or about things and people, always in a pleasant tone of voice and as if they were sitting a long ways away from each other.

Later, when I was a little older and Sofía began to teach me, I learned that she would spend all day searching for the way, the words by which to say things, taking into account, first and foremost, Sergio's anguish.

"We must control ourselves. Be aware, perfectly lucid, give facts, feelings, and thoughts their appropriate form, not let ourselves be dragged along by them, like most people do." Sergio would tell me about this in his letters from Europe, before he returned, and then it was a matter of adjusting everything to human proportions, because excess is always more powerful than man; it was a personal discipline, almost a game, but when he spoke to me about anguish, that it would enter his breast and not allow him to think or breathe, because it was slowly invading him, possessing him through that initial wound, like a cold knife in the chest, I understood that I should apply everything he had taught me about form to that, and so between the two of us we would search for mild words to warm the wound, and we forbade ourselves any expression of emotion, because the first shout would set the beast free.

Although at that time I was still going to school and visiting my cousins, I realized from the beginning that I shouldn't use my brother's and sister's language, nor ever allude to the conversations I heard at home. "Why don't they ever go to parties?" our relatives would ask me. "They shouldn't let themselves feel humiliated by Pablo's misfortune," they would add. I couldn't tell them that they didn't feel humiliated, that on the contrary, they were on the alert, and they couldn't waste a single instant of their attention, because they had to be on their guard precisely against that misfortune.

"No! Why Sergio? The doctor can say what he likes, because he's a pathetic, small-town physician. He tries to oversimplify everything; he thinks that what Sergio has is melancholia; he has no idea what anguish is.

"Sergio used to say, 'I'm looking for something tense and harmonic, on which my soul can slide. Not these peaks, these useless wounds, this falling down and picking yourself up; higher, lower, sideways, nearly motionless and dizzy. Do you see? I feel like I'm falling, like they're throwing me down inside, do you understand?—they throw me out of myself and as if I'm falling I can't breathe and I scream, and I don't know and I feel like they're knifing me, with a real knife, right here. I walk around with it stuck inside me, and I fall down and lie there motionless, I keep on falling, motionless, falling, nowhere, toward nothing. The worst part is that I don't know why I'm suffering, for whose sake, what I've done to deserve this huge remorse, that isn't caused by anything I could have done, but rather something else; and sometimes it seems like I'm finally going to reach it, finally to know, understand why I suffer so horribly, and when I concentrate hard and am about to reach it, and I hold out my chest, here comes the blow, the wound again, and I start falling again, falling. This is what they call anguish, I'm certain of that.'

"What does this have to do with melancholy? I can understand it, feel inside myself my brother's anguish when he speaks of falling and his fingers suddenly become icy and stuck to mine with the sweat of suffering, just like my mother's sweat that afternoon when I mopped her forehead and she couldn't feel it anymore. If anguish and gratuitous remorse are madness, everything is too easy and it's monstrously unfair that Sergio should suffer so much for nothing. Madness, then, would be a mere maladjustment, a silly thing, a slight detour in the road, barely perceptible, because it doesn't lead anywhere; a little like a quick sideways glance. That can't be. Why Sergio?

"He needs support. Something real, material, that he can cling to."

That's how Sofía invented the staircase, or rather, had Sergio invent it. She made them imagine it and then calculate, measure, step by step, the proportions, the terrain, the slope, the weight of the house, that should stay up there, solid, as if it and the stair-case were the same thing and could live each other's lives at the same time.

They were partly successful in their project. It's true that when you enter the house and cross the corridor and the hall for the first time, you stop at the edge of the stairway as if it were the edge of an abyss, with the minor terror of knowing that you might have taken one more, false, step. But after stifling that small scream that has never been heard and sounds more like a sudden catch-ing of the breath, all the visitors have tried to express surprise, not fear. Why fear? To be surprised is natural, since they didn't expect to find *that* there, that is, the patio that has been made into a staircase without anyone's knowing why, and, especially—they all say the same thing—since beauty and harmony are always surprising; they take your breath away. Beauty and harmony are what Sofía drew out of Sergio's anguish, so he would know that he had them, that they were inside him in spite of the anguish, but perhaps also to see them herself and give everyone palpable, ma-terial proof that her brother's mind worked better than the minds of the whole town combined; and it's true that they wouldn't have been able to create that lovely, smooth white slope that descends to the river's edge more elegantly than a hill. No, Sofía wasn't think-ing about the town; she had nothing to prove to the town; in fact, when they asked her about the staircase—what was it for?—she just shrugged her shoulders and ignored the question. Still, she never missed an opportunity for someone to come see the stair-case, and she would watch, always with great satisfaction, for the moment when they caught their breath.

Without opening my eyes I can see him, contemplate his slender body silhouetted against the arches. Still embroidering, I see him pretending to watch the men at work. He stares fixedly and I know that his hands are icy. It's five in the afternoon; the hour of the siesta is over, but he hasn't slept; it's been a long time since he's known what it is to sleep; he flings himself across the bed and stares at the ceiling with his eyes wide open and empty. It's five in the afternoon and it's June; the sun is still high and it falls across him with its obliterating light, with its shattering heat, but Sergio doesn't notice; he's standing there, pretending to be overseeing the workers, impeccably dressed in gray wool and a cravat. Such effort. Maybe that's what it consists of: pushing effort up against an absurd border, searching fiercely for what's on the other side of the border. He had to get out of bed, leave his room and inspect the work, he had to do it and he didn't forget it while he lay with his eyes fixed on the ceiling. How did he manage to remember it? How could he pull himself away from that place? Not even I know how hard that is for him every day, but he does it, and more, much more: he takes a bath, gets dressed, combs his hair, puts on perfume as if his date with that small duty were with duty personified. And now he's standing there, beaten down by the sun but unaware of it; that is, untouched, watching without watching. But tonight, when I ask him, beg him, order him to, he will know how far the work has come, how it got to that point, and if it's coming along well. Tomorrow morning I will make him go down to the river once more, again to figure out the problem of the sandy soil. It's cruel, cruel for me to watch him squint his eyes as if I were prodding him, watch him pressing his lips together, or keeping his forehead smooth through sheer willpower, to show me he isn't suffering. Yes, he keeps his brow smooth in order to reassure me.

"Sergio, if it's so easy for you to calculate, if you recognize it by just bending over and touching the soil, if watching the river makes you suddenly smile, even if just a little, why don't you do it always, every day?"

"No, you've got to understand, I don't want you to accept things the way they are, just because they're there; I want you to live among them, for that purpose, so that you can name them, can smile at them; Sergio: Look at me! . . . Forgive me, I know you recognize me, but it scares me, it scares me to death to think that someday you won't pay any attention to me, just like you don't pay attention to the trees or the bricklayers . . . and yet, at night, if I torment you, you know exactly what they've done and if they did it badly or well. It's another way of paying attention, you told me. What do you use to look with? . . . Sergio: look at me!"

Sofía was right in not permitting Sergio to be seen by the doctors. I don't know very much about your father; I didn't see him before it started or when it began. Maybe he was clinically a madman, but they knew so little about his illness that they let him come here and give it to his brother and sister who weren't like him, who were brother and sister to each other. Sergio went mad like your father did when he saw him, when he tried to understand. It isn't that he felt pity, foolish compassion; he just wanted to understand. But surely that is the road that madness itself has paved for its select few. One must hear the screams, the shrieks, without blinking, as Sergio did day and night. He should have thought about something else. Instead, Sergio listened attentively to the bestial shriek that filled the silence, that spread out over the surface of the night. Yes, I do know that: It didn't penetrate the night; your father's madness screamed at itself, not at anything else.

If we hadn't brought him home.... At least Sergio wouldn't have learned that scream. The one that was his downfall. The scream, the howl, the shriek that is hidden inside everyone, inside everything, without our knowing it.

I water the plants in slow motion every afternoon, so I won't disturb it, so it won't awaken inside Sofía, who now occupies the hand-carved room that once belonged to Pablo and Sergio. She hurls it out and listens to it; I keep watering my plants. I understand that she has to hurl it out, but I shouldn't try to understand it. I shouldn't for your sake, so you'll never have to come here, so you'll never feel obliged to keep this vigil that will end when there's no one left to resist for. Don't ever come here.

Even when they tell you that I stopped waiting, stopped being alert without giving in, even then, don't come. Don't try to understand. I'll tell you and only you that perhaps I've kept going because I suspect, with fear and trembling, that what we represent within the order of the world can be explained, but what we were meant to live through isn't fair, isn't human, and I, unlike my brother and sister, don't want to understand what's outside our little order. I don't want to, but nature is stalking me.

Because, really, to explain: What does a madman explain? What does it mean? It roars, scrapes the ground clean like a river, blindly drowns things in its waters, drags the lowing beasts along in an ancestral sacrifice, hallucinating, searching in its current for obliteration, for rest in a calm sea that will take no heed of its furious, destructive arrival. What sea?

It gathers up its fury in the high mountains: it fills up with wrath in the storms, in the snows that it never sees, that are not it; it is engendered by wind and water; it is born in canyons and has no memory of its birth.

The peace of an estuary, of a majestic flowing toward still depths. Never to stammer again, never to scream; to sing for a moment before entering immensity, in the eternal song, in the measured and eternal rhythm. Gradually to lose, along the banks, the fury of origins, to calm oneself beside the silent poplars, licking the solid earth, and to leave it, after barely touching it, to achieve the ultimate song, the imposing whisper of the final moment, when the sun becomes an equal, the pacified enemy of the immense waters ruling themselves.

Distrustful, cross with itself, an enemy of everything, it gives itself up at last, small and at peace, reduced to its own dimensions, to death. It scarcely learned to die by killing, for no reason, in order to achieve awareness of itself, in the instant immediately before breaking away from its origins, from the history it doesn't remember, peaceably powerful before giving in, tranquil and enormous, widened, imposing before the sea, which isn't expecting it, which murmurs indifferently and devours it without pity.

Water, simple water, muddy and clear, spiteful whirlpools and translucent pools, sun and wind, gentle stones at the bottom, like flocks of sheep, destruction, crimes, calm depths, fertile banks, flowers, birds and tempests, strength, fury and contemplation.

Don't leave your city. Don't come to the river country. Don't ever think about us, or about madness, again. And never let it cross your mind to love us a little.

The Silent Words

For José de la Colina

Names. They also enter the realm of mystery, they correspond to other things. That's how it was with Eduwiges. He couldn't settle for calling her Eluviques so he called her simply Lu, and lu is the name of a halftone on the Chinese musical scale: precisely the meaning and the sound that vibrated in him when he saw her move, with her tall, elastic young body over the tender, dark greens of his parcel of land, when he heard her laugh with her ringing laughter that set the birds fluttering.

She asked him once:

"If you know so many things, why don't we go away to the city? I know you have money saved up, but you're a tightwad. There are rich Chinese there, very rich, living in the lap of luxury. Open a store in Culiacán. I'll help you."

"Why do I live on the jade-green hill?

I laugh and don't respond. My serene heart:

a peach blossom carried off by the current.

Not the world of men,

I live under another sky, in another land."

"Go to hell. You and your foolishness."

But she had given him three children and had sung under the thatched roof.

Then there was that other business, too, the fact that Don Hernán, every once in a while, would speak seriously with him and, when he was in a good mood, would call him Confucius or Li Po. Don Hernán had traveled all over the world, read everything. And later, when the great persecution of the Chinese in the Northwest came, he hadn't allowed any of them to be touched, neither rich nor poor. And he had loaned him, surely on a whim, that book translated from the English, and Manuel had copied down the poems with such difficulty, because when it came to reading, he could read easily, but writing, he never had written since he had first learned how. Who was he going to write to? He wouldn't even have anyone to write to in Chinese, although he could have remembered enough characters to do it. "No more yearning to return / forgetting everything one has learned, among the trees." That's what he had decided when he arrived, how many years ago now? For that he has no memory. Yes, he does remember his teacher over there. The silence. . . .

"Manuel. I'm expecting visitors tomorrow. I want you to bring me some more poppies, but they have to be the very prettiest ones you have."

"Yes, yes." And he moves his head as if it were sitting there unattached atop his long, smooth neck.

"My parents-in-law are coming, you know. Well, the people who are going to be my parents-in-law. They're coming to ask for my hand."

"OK, OK, I give you flowells."

"Thank-you, Manuel. Oh! By the way, I'm going to invite you to the wedding."

"Good, very good."

He, too, had gotten married and Don Hernán himself had been his best man. Maybe that's why Don Hernán had felt obliged, when Lu went away with Ruperto, to send for him and tell him that they could make her come back, put her in jail, take her children away, they could . . . they could do so many things. . . . Don Hernán was angry.

No. He had always sold produce to Ruperto and he was an honorable man. Lu had given him happiness and three children. On those afternoons when Ruperto would go out with his truck, and they would carry the vegetables between the two of them, after they were finished, Lu would come up and offer them fresh fruit juice, as he had taught her to do, and it wasn't their fault if they knew how to laugh loudly at the same time, and to talk the same, with the same pronunciation, about the same things, standing there for a long time; he had seen it while he listened quietly. That went on for years. As for the children, those little untamed beasts . . . they were identical to her, even physically molded in her image. They had her big yellow eyes, although they were slightly slanted; furthermore, he had made every effort to teach them what he had learned when he was a child, as small as them, and they had only responded with indications of surprise. Astonishment, if not repudiation, is what he had felt in each of them when, at the right moment, he had taken them to see the San Lorenzo after the flood, majestic and calm, and in a low voice, playing with a leaf or caressing a stone, he had said slowly, "Far away, the river runs into the sky."

Despite his warnings, in the course of their games they trampled and destroyed the nursery beds, and he hadn't managed to get them lovingly to transplant a single little plant or to stand still for an instant, quietly watching something, for instance the moon, so strange and intimate.

It wasn't even people's names, the names of things, that escaped him, it was only their articulation. And that was all: enough for them to consider him inferior, everyone, everyone; at times, not even Don Hernán understood him fully, deeply. Only the other Chinese. Yes, it was not a coincidence that he didn't talk like the others, that he had his own special way of doing it.

> "Old ghosts, new ones
> Worry, crying, no one.
> Aged, broken,
> I sing only for myself."

The clarity was beginning. Emerging from silence, it

remains quiet for a while and touches things imperceptibly. Quietly.

It was the best time to dig his bare, shriveled foot into the spongy earth to feel, in the darkness, the first damp lettuce, which he didn't see but remembered from the day before, from so many days before when he already knew when it would be ripe; in order to cut it, noiselessly, with the sharp knife. And to stay here like this, relishing the silence of that thing that wasn't work but prophecy and knowledge. Then, stealthily, the light began to appear, until the birds awoke. "A rooster crows. Bells and drums on the river bank. One cry follows another. A hundred birds all at once."

He kept walking on his knees between the furrows, refining the words inside himself; there was no reason to stop. Meanwhile, he felt on his face, on his back, on his tranquil sides, how the deep breathing was beginning in the orchards surrounding his parcel. Forever dark and secret, closed in on themselves, the enormous orchards were beginning to stir. When the light had become too vivid, it was enough to lift his head a bit for his eyes to rest on the dark stain projected by the trees.

It was not time to cultivate, it was time to sell. Going into the bamboo-and-straw hut, forever cool under the great mango tree left in the middle of his tilled land, he eats something for breakfast and gets ready. He doesn't realize, maybe because no one, no one pointed it out to him, that he dresses the same as he did in his country, that the enormous, cone-shaped hat woven with his own hands isn't like the ones worn by the men in town, except, of course, for the other men of his race that live there. Careful to keep his balance, he lifts the two, very large, baskets, arranges the twine, adjusts them at either end of the long pole that he places across his shoulders, and lifts the weight as if he didn't feel it. He trots evenly along the edge of the canal crossing the orchard, then straight down the dusty path stretched among the fruit trees. He passes the big house and waves to the people strolling in the gardens, through the yards, without losing the rhythm of his little bird-hops.

From the time he reaches the first houses, without raising his voice too much, he begins to announce his wares.

"Vegetal, vegetal."

He knows it's *vegetables* but he can't pronounce it. There are so many things he'd like to say, he's tried to say, but he gave up because they sound ridiculous, they sound ridiculous to him in his stammering of a child that doesn't know how to talk yet. Only Don Hernán. . . . But with the others he doesn't insist; he understands that if you don't make yourself understood, other people think it useless to respond, to talk to you, because they feel you don't understand, that your inability to express yourself correctly is a sure sign of your incapacity truly to understand. He didn't feel rancor or get upset; he had known from childhood: "If we don't know the value of men's words, we don't know them." And he is a man, even though he's old, even though the inexplicable clumsiness of the roof of his mouth, of his tongue, forces him to resign himself to the simplest of interactions, and other people don't see him as he really is. They're fond of him, it's true; they ask him to do them favors and they do favors for him; but they don't talk to him like they do among themselves, even though some of them are so stupid.

"Manuel! Do you have any squash?"

"Manuel!"

How long has that been his name? How many years has he been in this town? How long ago was he born? There inside him, deep down, is his real name, but he hasn't told it to anyone. Not even secretly to Lu, whispering in her ear, many years ago.

He quickly finishes selling his produce and goes back to work.

Out back is the poppy bed. Beautiful to behold like no other. He thinks about the Englishman, about De Quincey, whose words he has copied, who never saw them in their winged splendor, filling the air with their fragile charm. It's February; in March he'll have to work at his private harvest of opium, but it isn't really work: it brings him pleasure, intense pleasure. While he prunes the plants, he watches them and listens to the sighs of unopened petals. He cuts a bud.

> "I'm not ashamed, at my age, to put a flower in my hair.
> The one ashamed is the flower crowning an old
> man's head."

In March, he harvested the double poppies, triple poppies, that people bought eagerly. But he saved the reserves and began distilling the thick juice from the heart of the flowers.

Every year he did this, and he secretly saved it for moonlit nights, lonely nights, or when he was going to converse, deliberately, with his own people.

In May, when the sun dazzles you, makes you sweat, but still doesn't weigh you down or put you to sleep, they arrived.

His three children and a stranger, in Ruperto's strong, modern truck:

"These young people are here to claim their inheritance, their right to your land . . ."

He didn't hear any more. He didn't want to hear more.

He looked at his tall, wild, alien children.

He knew that the land belonged to Don Hernán, who had given it to him to cultivate, so there would be vegetables, flowers in town, and that Don Hernán wasn't going to let anyone take a single dirt clod of this land away from him. But that wasn't the issue.

He waited till nightfall. Slowly, he began smoking his long pipe. There was no hurry. When he figured he was near paradise, he set fire to his bamboo hut, lay back down in bed, and kept on smoking.

Orphanhood

For Mario Camelo Arredondo

I thought it was all a dream: lying on a hard bed, covered with a very white sheet, was I, tiny, a little girl with my arms cut off above the elbows and my legs severed above the knees, dressed in a little white gown that exposed my four stumps.

The room where I lay was obviously a shabby examination room with old-fashioned windows. I knew we were alongside a highway in the United States where everyone in the world, sooner or later, had to pass by. And I say *we* were because standing next to the bed, in profile, was a cheerful, clean-cut young doctor. I waited.

My mother's relatives came in: tall, handsome, they filled the room with sunlight and chatter. The doctor explained to them:

"Yes, it's she. Her parents had an accident not far from here and they both died, but I was able to save her. That's why I posted the sign, so you would stop."

A very white woman, who reminded me vividly of my mother, caressed my cheeks.

"She's so pretty!"

"Look at those eyes!"

"And that curly blond hair!"

My heart raced with happiness. The moment of recognition had come and, amid those soothing words, there was no mention of my mutilation. The hour of acceptance had come: I was part of them.

But for some mysterious reason, in the midst of their laughter and chatter, they filed cheerfully out of the room and didn't look back.

Then my father's relatives came. I closed my eyes. The doctor repeated what he had said to the first set of family members.

"Why did you save *that thing*?"

"It's obviously inhuman."

"No, there's always something surprising, even funny, about a freak."

Someone short and strong grabbed me under the armpits and swung me around.

"You'll see, you'll find something else to do with her."

And he placed me on top of a sort of rail suspended between two brackets.

"One, two, one, two."

One at a time, he started pushing the stumps of my legs forward on that acrobat's prop, holding me up by the collar of my little nightgown like a grotesque doll. I shut my eyes tighter.

Everyone laughed.

"Obviously, there *is* something else you can do with her!"

"What fun!"

And, amid obscene horselaughs, they went away without my ever having looked at them.

When I opened my eyes, I awoke.

A deathlike silence reigned in the cold, dark room. There was neither a doctor, nor an examination room, nor a highway. I was here. Why did I dream about the United States? I'm in the windowless room of a building. No one came by nor ever will. Perhaps no one had come by before, either.

The four stumps and I, lying in a bed soiled with excrement.

My horrible face, nothing like the one in the dream: my features are shapeless. I know. I can't have a face, because no one ever recognized me nor ever will.

The Nocturnal Butterflies

For Ana and Francisco Segovia

For the heart whose woes are legion
'Tis a peaceful, soothing region—
For the spirit that walks in shadow
'Tis—oh 'tis an Eldorado!
But the traveller, travelling
    through it,
May not—dare not openly view it;
Never its mysteries are exposed
To the weak human eye unclosed;
So wills its King, who hath forbid
The uplifting of the fringéd lid;
And thus the sad Soul that here
    passes
Beholds it but through darkened
    glasses.

By a route obscure and lonely,
Haunted by ill angels only,
Where an Eidolon, named NIGHT,
On a black throne reigns upright,
I have wandered home but newly
From this ultimate dim Thule.

Edgar Allan Poe

When I saw him brush her cheek with the whip, I knew what I had to do.

It was strange, because he liked adolescents. This one was about eighteen.

In order to impress her, I arrived in the horse-drawn carriage from the very beginning. That didn't have the least effect on her.

I realized it was a difficult enterprise and I started visiting her every afternoon, at sundown. I would calculate when she would almost be through grading the homework of the fifth and sixth graders she was in charge of at Don Hernán's school. Sometimes there were good papers that she would hand me to read, radiant, and then I knew her vulnerable point. I liked to call on her.

I started loaning her books, which she would devour. Greek tragedies, novels by Musset, by George Sand ... in short, everything that occurred to me, art books, travel books.

Her oval face, with its delicate complexion, clouds over or lights up as she reads along. Because she doesn't pay any attention to me or stand on formalities. She reads or pores over the albums as if she were alone. Only when she needs me for something does she lift her dainty eyelids and ask. About France, India, Europe. Yes, I have been there with him, and in many other places, and I tell her all I can. How, with painstaking care, he has brought trees and birds from different places. I don't lose my patience: I am simply fulfilling my duty. Her tiny mouth, broad forehead, delicate nose, and enormous, black eyes may move many people, but not me. I won't allow it.

Someone has said something to her. I can tell from her reticence and lowered lids, from the absence of questions and interest for several days. But I've made up my mind; she has no parents, she's alone, it's very expedient.

Suddenly she begins asking me about the house on the hacienda. If it's true that there's an entire floor that serves as an enormous cage for little birds of every variety; about the pool, surrounded by Doric columns; about the flamingos, the peacocks, and the gardens.

This curiosity doesn't please me, and I bring her albums and more books. Now she falls into a long, drawn-out reverie as she contemplates or reads. She no longer asks me about anything. I believe the moment has arrived.

"Are you a virgin?"

"Yes."

"I'm prepared to offer you five hundred pesos in gold for your virginity. One night for two hours. Nothing more. You'll never be bothered again and no one will ever know. There's no danger of pregnancy."

"With him?"

"Yes."

"I don't want any money; I want to see the library and the paintings."

That was it. No bargaining with her parents. No crying or prudishness.

I took the carriage with just one horse, in order not to attract attention. I didn't turn on the headlights until we had left town. Then, when we reached the road through the orchards that leads up to the big house, I reined in the horse and climbed down to turn on the headlights. She didn't say anything. We went slowly on, at a walk, in the shadow of the great fruit trees stretching their branches over the dusty road. It was the beginning of a hot autumn, of course, but at midnight among the trees, there was a cool breeze arising from the sea. She crossed her arms over her chest but didn't say anything.

When we reached the gravel paths and the silhouette of the house stood out, imposing, against the night, she shuddered. It was all dark except for one window on the second floor, *her* window.

Meanwhile, I lit the porcelain oil lamp that I had already prepared. Holding the lamp up high, I guided her along. When we reached the hall, she saw the enormous, round marble table and the huge book with leather binding lying on it.

"What's that?"

"They're Don Hernán's memoirs, about his travels."

She walked over to the table and opened the handwritten book. She stood there reading it, turning pages as if she had come there for that purpose. I impatiently held up the lamp.

Then, as quickly as I could, I took her to the library. The same thing happened again. Slowly, she examined the shelves, taking down a volume and leafing through it. Finally, she said:

"There's lots of books in French and English."

"And in German and Latin. Let's get out of here."

She spent another eternity viewing the paintings. The *pursang* horses by George Stubb, Crome the Elder, with his Norfolk landscapes, Constable's *The Lock* . . . it was getting out of hand.

"They're not at all like the ones in the albums. They're something else altogether . . . ."

Before she could finish, I dragged her upstairs.

I ordered her to go into the room next to Don Hernán's, take off all her clothes, and put on the immaculate white robe that was always laid out for these occasions. First I peered under the door to make sure his light was on. It was. He must have smoked at least a pack of cigarettes, waiting. I gently coaxed her in and shut the door silently.

In the darkness, my eyes were burning.

My linen suit was sweaty and crumpled, but I couldn't even loosen my necktie: it wasn't permitted. Restless, I squirmed in the armchair; sitting in it all night was an unpleasant prospect. But I couldn't stand up, stretch my legs, make any noise. If I were a servant I could have taken a nap, but I'm not a servant. My watch, on those occasions, ended between one and two in the morning, and now day was dawning, but the door didn't open.

First the din of the birds began, then the mahogany of the staves and pillars began to shine, lustrous.

It didn't bring her out. Sitting in the gallery, next to her bedroom, I watched the sunlight streaming in.

I had no choice but to swallow and sweat my anxiety. What was happening? The rules of the game had been broken; rules I didn't invent, that I simply adopted as an adolescent.

Now the hustle and bustle of the household began. Singing. It was no longer possible to keep the secret. The rumor had spread, yes, but no one had seen it. People knew about it, because outsiders had witnessed it, but not a single servant in the big house could say, "I saw it." And now they would see it. But what could have happened inside there to annihilate all form? And what about me, didn't I count? He hadn't thought about me.

I didn't deserve such an affront. I had accepted his sporadic fancy for what he called "the holocaust of virgins," but only because he was a collector. He secured my services in order to compile his collection and that united us all the more.

On the other hand, if someone else had done it, he would have acquired a power different from mine. An intimacy that belonged to me.

"I am like the minotaur."

And I was the high priest.

Now I feared that something terrible might have happened. If she had died, he would know what to do. But what if he had died? . . .

My anxiety turned to anguish. I felt all broken up inside. I even remembered that my name isn't Lótar, that it was he who gave me that name.

The door opens and he calls me and has me go into the room. The first thing I see is the pile of ashtrays on his bureau, overflowing with cigarette butts.

As if it were the most natural thing in the world, he tells me,
"Lótar, this is Lía . . ."

"But . . ."

"She's Lía because she can't be Raquel. There is no Raquel
for me. I'll settle for Lía, so she can live with us."

"With us? . . . "

"Yes, tell her good morning, address her by name."

"—Good morning, Lía."

She smiled at me without a hint of shyness. Wrapped in
that lovely, white Japanese robe, with nary a wrinkle. Her smile
looked natural. She didn't realize what was happening. Or did she?

"Good morning."

Just like any other morning, I went into the adjoining
bathroom to draw the bath.

While I was washing him in the hot tub, and afterward,
massaging him, he was totally distracted. We returned to the bedroom. She was sitting still in a Regency chair. He turned his back on
her, and I could feel him hardening, coming back to himself, while
I filed his nails and made them shine. Then he wandered around
distractedly, apparently searching for a spot where Lía wouldn't
be able to see him, and he untied the belt of his bathrobe. I went
over immediately to dress him. I believe I always knew what he
wanted to wear, but this time he had me take him three or four
different outfits. He was in the habit of pacing and talking while I
dressed him, but today he seemed riveted to one spot, giving the
curtest orders about his clothes. I could barely make out the nape
of Lía's neck, so fragile.

"Open the shutters."

The day rushed into the bedroom with its full weight. Its
light had the burning hue of honey.

"Take her away. Show her to her room. The one with the
other marble bathtub."

When I returned, I began dressing him in silence.

He was pacing the room, as usual.

He ordered me to bring the storage trunks just as they
were, because he, personally, wanted to pick out the fabrics and
patterns that Adelina would use to start Lía's wardrobe, beginning with a dress for that afternoon. Poor Adelina, what with all
the lace edging and braiding he had selected for that one pattern.

"She won't come to the table with the guests yet. I need you to teach her how to eat; in short, teach her the customs of this house. You won't come to dinner or supper either, because you'll have to eat with her on the western terrace. After everyone else leaves, the three of us will meet. And you'll send for Monsieur Panabière."

And he went on talking to me about the dogs, the birds. He sent for the chef and, as usual, discussed with him what we would have for breakfast, dinner, and supper that day.

Then he told me: "Find Lía a lady's maid who will know how to dress her, to do her hair right. Even if it's someone who's otherwise employed. We'll replace her later."

Panabière arrived and Don Hernán shut himself away with him for the rest of the morning.

Lía's life wasn't what I had imagined. She was being educated in the strictest of disciplines and she submitted to it: at seven in the morning she had to be up and dressed, so Pablo, the head groom, could teach her to ride horseback; then a bath, and dressing again for breakfast with me, and entire mornings shut up with Monsieur Panabière in the library. Then dinner and an hour of rest. But she didn't rest: all alone, she would cross the garden and venture into the shady orchards, next to the San Lorenzo River, where everything was humus, fallen leaves from the mangos, the litchi trees, the cuadrados and the caimitos. What did she do during those hours, when we were all taking our oppressive siesta? Sometimes she would carry a book in her hand, but other times she wouldn't take anything with her. Despite my curiosity, I never dared follow her. Next would come the English class, with Mr. Walter, a machinist at the mill, and then Don Hernán himself would teach her how to stand, walk, nod acknowledgments, charmingly, without uttering a word. He signaled her gently with his whip: on the waist, on the shoulders, on her legs covered with rags; he had her try on elaborate dresses, with trains, so she could learn how to move gracefully in those reams of cloth. Then another bath, and supper with me. At night she would study. I would see a light on in her room until early morning. But she didn't complain.

At first, when we would dine alone together, she tried to continue our afternoon conversations, but I refused, I would scarcely answer her, and from that moment on, though she was always on my mind, I observed her and spoke to her as little as possible. Even now I don't know who she was, or what she was like, or why she did what she did.

She was all alone.

The first shock to the town came one Sunday. Don Hernán arrived in the open carriage with the parasol held over his head, together with me and Monsieur Panabière, for the eleven o'clock mass, the only mass of the day. We went in the great carriage with four horses. I have to admit she was very beautiful, crisp in her white dress, even in August.

The priest had to pretend he believed she was a relative of Don Hernán's, though he knew perfectly well what people were saying.

She sat down with Don Hernán in the first pew, which, like the prie-dieu, was lined with velvet. Monsieur Panabière and I sat in the second row. Each pew had a little metal plaque that said in gold letters, "Fernández Family." No one sat in those two pews when Don Hernán wasn't there, even when the chapel was overflowing.

People watched the family members curiously, as if for the first time.

What impressed Lía was the music. In those days you could still hear Bach played in church. The organist was a nun from the town's private school.

There wasn't any real problem. Don Hernán went in person to speak with the mother superior and everything was arranged.

Lía was to study whatever the little nun would teach her on the grand piano.

When Pablo told Don Hernán she was an absolute amazon, that she knew how to jump, could master the most spirited of horses, serene and confident in the saddle, Don Hernán already knew it. He sent for the lovely riding outfit with Frederick boots, the embossed saddle with her name, Lía, hand tooled on it, of course. Then he took her out to a little corral where there was only one horse prancing about, a *pur-sang*: Edgar, since everything must make sense. She adored Edgar from the very beginning.

From then on she would ride alone, independently. She would cross the village and venture into Callejón Viejo, lined with bamboo trees so tall that they came together at the top to form a canopy. "Like a Gothic cathedral," he used to say. She would charge through the sugar mill and distillery like a bolt of lightning, because they didn't interest her. Then she would venture into the thickest part of the cane fields, surrounded by guava trees, with signs reading, "Traveler: the fruit is yours. Be kind to the tree." For some strange reason everyone seemed to understand it, even if they didn't know how to read, and the rule was observed.

And time went by.

One morning Don Hernán surprised me:

"I want Lía, naked, in the Japanese robe."

I didn't expect that. Lía had grown, she was a woman. Not his cup of tea at all, although, since she had arrived, he had not requested adolescents again. He settled for me. And now ... suddenly ...

I felt afraid and, around dusk, I cracked the French doors open to watch, from the balcony, what was happening inside.

I delivered the message to Lía; she trembled slightly but accepted.

The preparatory ritual was the same as ever, and I ran to the balcony to spy on them.

The room was lit by two oil lamps and Lía stood in the middle of the room, passively naked. Her white body gleamed in total, mysterious perfection. Don Hernán took the great chest out of the safe and tried a ruby choker on her, then he slowly added pearls, sapphires, emeralds. At times he wouldn't like how something looked and he would trade it for another necklace, until her chest was covered, then her waist, then her sex. She didn't move; she was a statue. He stood there contemplating her for a long time and experimented with the light of the oil lamps, moving them from one spot to another and making the precious stones sparkle at different angles. When he liked an angle, he would lean back on his bed and lie there gazing at her for what seemed like forever. Then he would slowly begin unfastening the necklaces.

"Put on your robe and go to bed."

That was it.

But he had put his mother's jewels on her, and he had adored her, despite what they said.

He swore that none of his brother Fernando's descendants would ever use them. He utterly despised Fernando. His mother had lived for years in the Spanish court and there, amid scandal, she had borne a son to Alfonso XIII. Don Joaquín, her father, had recognized the son at birth, but being a Bourbon didn't prevent the child from being a bastard. Don Hernán allowed Fernando to live in great luxury in the European courts, but his coming to Eldorado would be something else again. He couldn't bear to look at Fernando.

A few days later, her introduction to society. All the high-ranking employees were invited, along with their wives. The general manager, Don Rodrigo de Quiroga, descendant of Don Vasco (every chance he got he clarified that his ancestor was already a widower when he took holy orders), was the first to arrive, with his stunning wife. The others arrived immediately afterward. Punctuality was an indispensable courtesy. Only Don Francisco Almanza, the field manager, came alone, but Don Hernán knew him well and greeted him more warmly than ever.

When everyone had gathered over a glass of sherry, she appeared. Don Hernán introduced her simply: "Ladies and gentlemen, this is Lía." The gentlemen stood up and, one by one, they told her their names. She half smiled at each of them. As for the ladies, she greeted them with a nod and a small, almost imperceptible bow.

Then we went into the dining room. The one who livened things up or told anecdotes or serious stories was Monsieur Panabière, who had come to the house for that purpose. For that purpose, to take care of the library and talk to Don Hernán. Lía would chime in, make observations, and Monsieur Panabière would watch her, mesmerized.

Everyone, especially Don Francisco, was friendly and charming toward her; and the ladies seemed taken aback but content. It was all very easy.

Lía would enliven the gatherings with simple but clearly phrased musical pieces with a certain, special feeling. Then she proceeded to play Chopin, Bach, Beethoven, Mozart, and that made everyone happy except me.

At night, Don Hernán would call me to his room, but it was rarely for that purpose, and when it did happen it was without passion, like a necessary, mechanical thing. Most of the time it was for me to sit quietly in the little Regency chair while he read and smoked one cigarette after another in his cigarette holder. I couldn't move. He would read until early morning and then fall asleep, the book still in his hands and the cigarette between his fingers. He was afraid, terrified, that one day he might set the bed on fire. That's what I was there for, to put out the last cigarette and take the book out of his hands.

Since Don Hernán didn't like to see people sweat, especially during meals, Clarisa would rub Lía with toilet water, dress her in gauze slips, and cover her with long, fanciful robes designed expressly for that purpose. Everything in white. No one showed any surprise and soon all of us, who were only men, got used to seeing her in that intimate attire.

One night during my watch, Lía came up to the big window. She watched the sky turn violet, then purple.

"They're burning the cane fields! I want to see it, from up close!"

It was nearly an order. She had them hitch up the large carriage and the buggies, and all the male dinner guests went into action.

We reached the first field they were burning. The flames had already reached the middle of the plantation. She sat there, absorbed, for a long time, ignoring other people's stares. Then, when least expected, she told one of the fieldworkers who had come up to watch Don Hernán's arrival:

"Cut me some sugarcane."

The worker obeyed.

"Would you like me to skin it, señorita? It's very hot."

"No, give it to me just like that."

And she sank her teeth into the cane, savored it, and kept on chewing while the juice ran down onto her billowy dress.

When she finished, everyone laughed heartily: she really

looked comical with her face all covered with soot and sugar-cane juice. She smiled. Everyone laughed loudly again, everyone but me. Don Hernán walked up to her very slowly and with his big, fancy-edged raw-silk handkerchief, he stood there meticulously wiping her face, content. While he did so, Lía's eyes flashed mysteriously, like the burning cane field.

The trip came a long time later.

In Switzerland, Don Hernán selected thirty-six white dresses for Inés Almanza, his favorite goddaughter, who must have been about seven then. He called her "the queen of the guava groves."

Of course, we went to Brussels, to the Hague, and that's where my captivity began: Lía wanted to go to all the museums, to the private houses that had famous paintings, and I was in charge of taking her, of getting permission, while Don Hernán would read back in the hotel or bask in the sun in some café. . . . He knew it all so well by then. . . . We went through Luxembourg and the same thing happened.

But Paris was the worst. We went to the Louvre every single morning.

Our first visit was with Monsieur Panabière, but that was enough to orient her and, anyway, Panabière was getting old and tired.

So it was up to me, following Don Hernán's orders.

We would begin, each day, by contemplating the *Victory* statue from Samothrace, for as long as she liked. She would call it familiarly *The Samotas*. And we would go back to see the museum, time and again, painting by painting, sculpture by sculpture.

Then we would eat with Don Hernán and Panabière and they would talk interminably about those art objects. Afterward, I also had to take her to the dressmaker's so she could try on ten thousand frocks that Don Hernán had selected for her in the morning; then we would order and pick up the jewels. It seemed natural to Don Hernán that I should carry out all those little additional errands, running back and forth, in spite of my fatigue. One afternoon she dragged all of us to the *vernissage* of a fellow named Degas: Oh! How marvelous! the ballerinas in their tutus; and the play of light . . .

When she had seen it all, she faced Don Hernán solemnly and simply said:

"I want the *Three Russian Ballerinas*."

Why that rough sketch, when there were so many exquisite things? But he didn't listen and went straight to the *marchand* to buy the drawing.

In Paris she realized that I was always left alone at night, bored and alone, waiting up for them, for the ritual of the book and the cigarette.

I don't know what she told Don Hernán, because it had been the same on all of our trips, but I know she was the one who did it. I was to go out with them from now on, he told me, like Monsieur Panabière. He ordered appropriate clothes to be made for me.

We went to the inauguration of the first air show and to see Farman and Blériot take off on their initial flight *ville à ville*.

Lía had an insatiable appetite for movies. Don Hernán had seen them before, in the United States, where he and I went in 1905. But none of us knew any more about it than what he would tell us over dinner, back at Eldorado, with its light and heat. We saw *L'assassinat du duc de Guise*, *L'avare*, *Le raid Paris-New York*, but Lía preferred Italian films. Afterward, dinner at Maxim's.

We went to see the Eiffel Tower and Lía didn't show the least surprise, and when Don Hernán suggested they go up, she said:

"I'd rather see everything from below."

And in Paris she dragged me from *quartier* to *quartier*, street to street, house to house, fountain to fountain, even including the suburbs. I couldn't take any more. I don't think she even slept, because she would buy books and more and more books in English and French, by the latest authors, and she would read all the newspapers to plan our activities for the afternoon and evening.

We would also go to the opera, to concerts followed by supper at Maxim's, until she got bored and said:

"I want to go to another restaurant." Then Don Hernán proposed La Tour d'Argent: we four and the Petitjeans.

I was stunned by the splendor of that place. They seated

them in two tête-à-têtes put together, and Monsieur Panabière and me in an adjoining one.

I felt comforted by the soft-white oil lamps, with little rococo flowers, that cast an intimate light, very like the light back home, and I paid no attention to what Monsieur Panabière was saying to me. I slowly sipped the champagne cocktail that Don Hernán had ordered for me.

But I did see it when Lía rudely stood up and walked over to us, asking the waiter for another stool. We both stood up and she sat down in my place, next to Panabière, and said:

"Describe it to me. From the beginning."

Monsieur Panabière started over again: the first thing you can't help but notice is the great, thousand-faceted chandelier in the entrance. All the decor is Louis XVIII. It's an attempt to reproduce the atmosphere of Madame Recamier's salon, that so many musicians, writers, and poets passed through. The ceiling was painted by Lully and represents the Trianon. That enormous cushion in the center and the green plants are in the same Empire style, as are the parquet and the large rug; the velvet curtains with gold braid are frayed with age. In the four corners are sketches that, from afar, look like water paintings, just like the ones at Versailles; also, the door is painted for the same effect. The tapestries are a true copy of the ones of the Lady-and-the-Unicorn. The mirrors, clouded with age, are designed to elicit the orange-tree path you saw in Versailles. La Tour's tower itself is one of only four towers that existed in Paris before the Revolution; that's why it reminds one of the Bastille. That ancient marble chimney, that isn't used because it would be hazardous to the visitors' health....

Don Hernán got up and said: "Let's go to the other room for supper."

I scarcely heard Monsieur Panabière murmur, "it's Louis XVI ... " We went in. I saw the heavy furniture and the still lifes. When we sat down I noticed that Don Hernán's chair was larger and had arms. On his right he seated Señora Petitjean and on his left Lía, next to Petitjean. Then us.

He saw the menu and turned to Monsieur Panabière:

"Order:
Homard à la gelée au champagne

with Liebfraumilch
Brioche de foie gras frais
with des Chateaux de la Loire rosé
Sole de ligne à la Daumont
with Vouvray white wine
Feuillete aux champignons du Jura
with Saint Emilion red wine
Perdreaux rôtis sur canapé
with Chateauneuf-du-pape red wine
Foie de canard aux olives vertes et noires
with Chateau-Chalon yellow wine
Arlequinade de sorbets
with Heidsieck champagne
Timbale Elysée
with the same champagne
Bond glacés
and let's continue with the champagne."

She asked:

"Don Hernán, you speak excellent French. Why don't you order?"

"When have you ever seen kings speak to foreign servants in their own language? That's what interpreters are for. Kings only speak other people's languages when they're among equals."

We barely tried the dishes and the wines. When they would remove the plates, they had hardly been touched. At the end of the meal, after his first glass of champagne, Monsieur Panabière fell into a deep sleep. Lía didn't keep on drinking, but the rest of them did, until they got loudly euphoric. I was all alone.

She fell in love with Italy.

Especially Florence, which she called "the perfect city." In all the years I knew her I only saw her cry once: before Rembrandt's self-portrait that hangs in the Uffizi Gallery. The tears rolled down her face, her own eyes fixed on those of the self-portrait.

We saw all of Florence on foot, as she preferred, museum by museum, street by street, house by house. She loved hearing stories of the Medicis. Meanwhile, Don Hernán would wait for us, sipping coffee or visiting shops and the Ponte Vecchio to buy more clothes and jewels for Lía. We stayed there three weeks.

Next she wanted to see all of Tuscany: Assisi, Pisa, Siena . . . and we would stay in each of those cities for at least three or four days, even if the inn wasn't as comfortable as Don Hernán would have liked.

And the olive trees all along the road, during our hours and hours of weary travels.

"Here in Europe the trees are much smaller than back home," she said. And she and Monsieur Panabière had a friendly argument about Europe and America.

In Rome, we kept up the same fast trot, so very fast, with me lagging behind. In Venice we spent our time in churches, museums, and lovely gondolas. In the *vaporetti* I would drowse, all worn out.

In Vienna, as usual, she never tired.

She was very surprised to see Moctezuma's headdress there and she stood for a long time contemplating Titian's *Dánae*. The city charmed her. We went to concerts. She could never get enough.

"Except for Bach, Beethoven, and Kant, all the great German artists have been Austrian. Isn't that right, Señor Panabière?" she said one night at supper.

"That's true," the old man replied.

All she wanted to see was the Rhine, the Black Forest. We passed through Berlin to see the Nefertiti. Thank goodness she didn't like that city. Anyway, she didn't speak German.

Then the Orient: India, which I had already visited, like everywhere else, and now I had to show it to Lía. She discovered that at Eldorado the top bosses dressed like Englishmen did in India, and it was true, a *sarakof*, boots or gaiters, very special linen suits. But there the jackets were more varied, more individualized. She was right.

What she liked the most, I think, was Indochina and the fabulous South Sea Islands. "The land of Lord Jim," she would say to Panabière, pleased as punch, and we traveled upriver in homage to something I didn't understand, the two of them whispering to each other, relishing their complicity. She would lean over and share the pleasures of that complicity with Don Hernán.

In Australia she asked for parakeets of every color, and Don Hernán, who knew how to please her by then, indulged her.

We were in Japan for two months. In Kyoto, because Lía liked it more than Tokyo; although we did go to Tokyo often to see performances, including at the Noh and Kabuki theaters. Even though Japan had opened up to the Western world twenty years earlier, don Hernán had never seen Japan.

Lía would carefully observe the customs.

One morning, when Don Hernán, already anxious to leave, called her in, she arrived taking tiny steps, completely dressed as a Japanese woman, but without any make-up. She made the inevitable curtsies, and in her best French she bade him a good morning with a long speech evoking cherry trees in blossom, although it was autumn.

Then she said to Don Hernán:

"I have a humble request."

Don Hernán responded, "Speak."

"I want to go to the mixed baths. The ones where men and women bathe together."

His face lit up even more.

"Granted."

And we went. They looked at us in surprise but said nothing. He didn't bathe, he simply stood there watching: all the Japanese men and women looked at her furtively. Perhaps they admired her? She swished around and, out of the corner of her eye, she didn't miss a single alteration in Don Hernán's expression.

And other requests followed: for Don Hernán to visit a geisha house and then tell her what it was like. He relished the idea.

She waited up for him, dressed in her most beautiful kimono, until after midnight. When he arrived she assaulted him with questions, but she didn't need to, he was taking great delight in it. He sat up till dawn telling her everything he had seen there, point by point, including the most intimate sexual details. I felt very annoyed.

At daybreak she told us to wait a minute, and poor Clarisa appeared with a perfectly arranged table service, and Lía performed the tea ceremony in all its ritual. Her hands seemed to move slowly and serenely through the service, but actually it was the precision of each movement that imposed that calm rhythm on her rapid actions. Her eyes were turned downward, but suddenly, on two occasions, she looked up directly at Don Hernán, with a steady, intense expression I couldn't describe, and I remembered having often seen her look at him that way.

"Perfect," he said.

That night we didn't get a wink of sleep.

Lía—who was all over the place, with me trotting behind her short little, rapid steps, the steps of a Japanese woman—took an interest in miniature gardens, and by asking around she found a botanist who specialized in grafting.

"That's what we need at Eldorado."

And for a small fortune, the Japanese man was hired.

That's also where we got the Japanese cherry trees that are red like the others when they mature but that have a delicate fuzz like peaches. They're still there, at least at Pedro Carreón's house.

When it started snowing we all had to buy winter kimonos. I felt ridiculous.

Then she got it into her head to go to China.

"At twenty below zero?" I said, stupefied.

"Empress Tz'u-hsi proclaimed a constitutional regime two years ago because the Nationalists were rebelling and now, in 1908, they're going to declare her four-year-old son, P'u-i, emperor. I want to see how a child that age wears a crown. I want to witness the ceremony. And anyway, because of the Russian-Japanese War, China has opened itself to the world like Japan for the first time."

I was overwhelmed.

And naturally, we went to China.

Those greatcoats weighed at least two tons. Even in the most elegant hotel there was no heat, only coal chimneys. She bought me "Japanese heaters" to warm up my hands.

With difficulty we managed to reach the Great Wall. It was curious. Now it was she who was the guide, who explained everything to us. He would listen to the explanations and I, lagging behind, would feel supremely bored and could find no way to warm myself. Monsieur Panabière was secretly enjoying it.

In China those days, everything had a price tag. That's how we were able to attend the famous coronation. That part did interest me. The Manchus followed their ancestral rituals, strange yet very beautiful.

It was Lía who selected the souvenirs, the gifts, the objects for the big house.

The English ship that took us to Hawaii was so restful! I could stretch out in the wicker chairs all day and sleep.

It was only at night that I had to perform the ancient rite with the cigarette and the book. And sometimes . . . he wanted me to pretend I was a geisha and I would despair.

In Hawaii—at long last!—sun, heat.

But unfortunately we weren't there for long. Then the English ship and those damned nocturnal rituals once again.

He didn't want me in the dining room, so they served me the finest foods in my cabin.

The cold once again, but more human this time.

And the nocturnal rituals that grew more and more complicated.

In Los Angeles he had a lot of friends and he and Lía devoted themselves to their social life.

"Lía speaks English too perfectly for these people who mangle their words," he told me one morning while I was bathing him. I didn't see her in action, didn't know anything about her activities and her latest tricks.

We returned via the South Pacific, comfortable and cozy, but without any bathtubs or showers, so we all had to settle for frequent rubdowns with toilet water. It was a long voyage.

Clarisa adored Lía and somehow made her clothes look as if they were always freshly ironed.

The Japanese man rejoined us before we crossed the border.

When we got home there was a big reception. Everyone was there, bosses and employees, fieldworkers, women with babies, the Chinese. No one worked that day. We had been away for nearly two years.

After making a big display of passing out gifts, Don Hernán set about arranging his books in the office, while Lía played hooky from her classes with Monsieur Panabière, who had been so obliging on the trip and now positively spoiled her.

She was continually running to the hothouse to see the Japanese man. And that resulted in the mango-pineapple tree, the perón-mango tree, the pear-mango tree, and those hybrid flowers that astonished everyone and gave Don Hernán such pleasure.

One afternoon, while enjoying a cup of coffee, we heard a loud, very familiar noise.

"It's the San Lorenzo flooding," he said.

She sat there without saying a word, then stood up and left the house. At a sign from Don Hernán, I followed her.

She crossed the orchards and stood contemplating the powerful river as it dragged along cattle, trees, branches. And, along its banks, aquatic plants and slime.

As if hypnotized, she started walking into the mud on the bank, into the weeds, into the slime. She sank in until she was covered with all those things up to her head.

"Lía! . . . Lía!" I shouted desperately. But the strong current drowned out my cries.

Then she came out, dripping, covered with mud, hair disheveled and crowned with filth. She was wearing one of the most expensive dresses we had bought in Paris, which was totally ruined now.

When we went back and Don Hernán saw her in that condition, he asked what had happened. I explained to him, indignant.

He laughed loudly, with great gusto, and said:

"What a brave girl."

That was all.

On another occasion I was surprised to see her opening the cage of the green Australian parakeets.

"They can survive. They look like leaves."

And that's what happened. Even today, over the ruins of Eldorado, you can see great flocks of them flying.

But one night, Don Hernán asked me to take Lía to him, observing all the protocol for the ceremony of the Minotaur.

Just like during her second visit, I took my precautions with the peepholes in the shutter. It was very strange, because Lía was a full-grown woman by now. This was really dangerous. She was just one step away—a step she might take that very night—from becoming the absolute sovereign.

When I told him that, he answered:

"That's fine," and smiled a triumphant smile.

That night, like every other, Lía stood there nude, looking like a statue. Around her neck he fastened a necklace made up of some of the emeralds bought on the trip. The usual ritual was beginning. But when he approached her directly to put another necklace on her, the statue suddenly moved and its arms encircled Don Hernán, drawing him toward it. An infinite moment went by in which they didn't move, then he pushed her violently away, throwing her backward. When she had regained her footing, she cast him a cold, disdainful look, tore the necklace off and threw it in his face. The blow blinded him and he covered his eyes with his hands. He recovered almost immediately and hurried over to where he had left the whip at bedtime; running with it held high in the air, he angrily stormed across the room. She stood there like a gleaming statue. He held the whip up level with her face. Then the arm clutching it fell, unhinged.

They stood still again, petrified. After a long time he said, in his usual authoritarian voice:

"Go to bed."

I have to admit that Lía restored my place in the house. I was the only one to see her leave that night, with her head held high, her hands empty, marching out the front door.

The Brothers

For Susana Crelis

As a young girl, I was walking along nearly blinded by the noonday sun. Suddenly, on the narrow sidewalk I saw his boots blocking my path. I looked up and there were his eyes like honey-colored embers. It was inexplicable: I wasn't a brave woman— barely more than a shapeless child—and I was shy. Yet both of us felt the electricity that threw us up against each other like two metal plates. Although there was nothing to stop us, we knew that that thing smelled like blood and death and had nothing to do with engagements and orange blossoms. But he didn't leave me with child because he took pity on me.

I grew up in another town. My eldest brother gave me a little stuffed lizard. Slightly over half a meter long. It was wonderful to look at it and think about my brother's great affection.

A well-dressed, handsome boy fell in love with me and I with him, as it is meant to be.

Our wedding day came, and when we got home from church, my brother silently led me to my bedroom and, from across the room, he pointed at the lizard. The right side of its face was exposed, spilling its eye onto its forehead, giving it a depraved look from the forehead to the snout. I don't know why I remembered the boy in boots and started trembling with fear.

All the guests came in and noticed the lizard's expression. I wrapped it up in a big bedspread, to avoid touching it, and went running to the sacristy in my wedding dress. The priest could not make out the words I stammered. Everything was mixed up.

The younger brother of the boy in boots inched his way in. No one recognized him but me. He placed his hand on my shoulder and fastened his calm eyes on mine. Approaching the table where the lizard lay, he began to caress it tenderly, firmly but tenderly, from head to tail. He protected the lizard's crest with his hand, but he kept on stroking it, his hand moving the length of the dead, angry animal. After a while, one by one or in clusters, the guests who had followed me there started drifting back to the party, bored; but not even my husband could make me budge from that spot where I stood hypnotized.

Time went by and the boy's strokes continued patiently over the stiff back. My groom and my brother stayed by my side.

Three hours later, when the drunken shouts were starting to drown out the music, the animal started gradually losing its smirk, resuming its normal expression. There it lay and no one wanted to pick it up.

The brother of the boy in boots came slowly toward me and, as he walked by, he said calmly:

"There won't be any blood shed."

The Mirrors

In memory of my grandmother,
Isabel Ibarra de Arredondo

"They've kidnapped La India!" shouted Mercedes, panting and running full tilt into the house.

Francisco rushed out of his office and over to Mercedes, who had slowed to a lope.

"What are you saying, child? Who kidnapped her? When?"

"They kidnapped her! They kidnapped her!"

He took her by the shoulders and shook her, telling her in an authoritative voice, "Calm down." Then he yelled to the first person within earshot, "Bring a glass of wine!" I was there by then, since the uproar had also brought me out of my room, and I walked quickly over to her.

While Mercedes moaned and tried to catch her breath, Francisco guided her to the nearest chair, patting her gently on the back. He sat her down and waited while she sipped the wine I fed her a little at a time, between sobs.

By then everyone in the household was present; that is, the servants and some of the farmworkers. Francisco told them to go back to work, except for Pablo and Chico.

"Let's take it slowly. When did they kidnap La India?"

"Just now! Just now!"

"Who?"

"Two men on horseback."

"Did anyone see them?"

"We all saw them. They were wearing serapes and hats, and had handkerchiefs over their faces. My mother is beside herself!"

"How did they kidnap her?"

"She was coming home from Concha's house when they rode by at a full gallop—oh, another drink, please!"

"So they rode by at a full gallop, and then what?"

"It was horrible! Dreadful!"

"What happened?"

"One of them rode up to the sidewalk and—whether you want to believe it or not—he grabbed La India by the waist, lifted her up on his horse and kept right on riding alongside the other horseman. Oh, I'm going to faint! This just can't be happening! It can't!"

"Bring a little glass of sherry and a big cup of lemon-grass tea. You two, Pablo and Chico, saddle up your horses and go get Emilio and the car. Someone had to have seen them, dressed like that."

"But it's dark now. If it happened a while ago, like she says, it must have been at sundown," I said.

"It doesn't matter. They can't have gotten far, and two horsemen riding at a full gallop can't help but attract attention."

"But Francisco, where are you going?"

"Outside, to ask around."

"What about La India's honor? If people find out she was kidnapped . . . "

"We'll just ask if anyone saw the horsemen. You stay here and make sure that no one leaves the house, and tell them you'll kill them if they breathe a word."

The group began to scatter, and then we heard the sound of hooves and, what seemed even stranger, loud laughter coming from the street. Temporarily dumbfounded, we all fell silent and still.

Isis, dressed like a man, with a handkerchief tied around

her neck and wearing a broad-brimmed hat, as was my son Rodrigo, who was with her, came in dragging two blankets on the ground. La India was doubled over in laughter, as were her two companions.

Blood rushed to Francisco's face; he clenched his teeth. His blue eyes flashed severely, menacingly, and without a word he stomped off to his office, pushing anyone who blocked his path out of the way. The pranksters and La India managed to get hold of themselves, but Rodrigo said, still laughing:

"Why make such a big deal out of an innocent joke? La India was really scared when we kidnapped her, but we took off our masks right away and then she had as much fun as we did. You know what the first thing she said was? 'They kidnapped me because I'm the prettiest girl in the Astorga family.' You should have heard Isis's retort, 'That's a lie; I'm the prettiest.' By the time La India said that, we had slowed down the horses, but Isis, furious, whipped her horse so hard that—"

"Rodrigo," I interrupted, "You've made a serious error in judgment. Doña Petra is beside herself and we've had quite a scare, all over nothing."

"Mama, Doña Petra has already seen that La India's back. She threw her arms around her, in tears; then, when she turned around and saw our disguises, she had a good laugh."

"Like mother, like daughter," I said.

"Doña Isabel," Isis protested, "nothing happened. It was just a game! And games are for amusement."

"A game? Do you think you have the right to entertain yourselves at the expense of those who love you?"

"We didn't stop to think about that, believe me. All at once the idea occurred to us and we just did it."

"Rodrigo, come talk to your father early tomorrow morning. No, maybe you'd better come in the afternoon, to give him a chance to calm down a little. As for me, I don't want to lay eyes on you for at least a week."

"But mama, please, forgive us, I'm sorry if we've upset you . . ."

"I'll try to find it in my heart to forgive you, over the next few days."

That night Francisco didn't come to dinner. I sat at the table and waited for him in vain, he who was always so punctual for meals. At ten I had the table cleared; I had been waiting for him two hours. As always, I made the rounds to see that all the doors in the house were locked. I walked into the bedroom and lay down, unable to sleep, and in the utter stillness of the night, I heard his footsteps pacing endlessly back and forth in the office. I don't know when I fell asleep, in the light from the bedroom lamp.

The next day, as usual, I got up at five in the morning to oversee the milking, and there he was, lying at my side, fast asleep.

The corrals took up the back of the house, to one side of the barnyard where we kept the geese. I saw the enormous tree, the mango, standing there like an old friend and, for some reason, that calmed me. As usual, I gave all the orders: for breakfast to be made, the dogs to be tied up; in short, for the house to run smoothly. At seven I heard Francisco taking a shower; then Natalia shaved him. The breakfast table was set. When we sat down I saw he was solemn but calm.

"Those Astorgas are very good girls, but they'll do anything for a laugh. They take after their father and mother. Just imagine Marcial—may he rest in peace—deciding to call his daughter Isis; that gives you some idea of what sort of fellow he was, and you know what Petra is like . . . "

"Let's not talk about it now, Isabelita. Just don't forget that Rodrigo is incredibly happy with Isis. As I think I mentioned, Isis is the name of an ancient goddess and Marcial was a real history buff."

"Like you."

"Even more so. He was really into mythology. Now let's forget about all this. Let's talk about what we have to do today, like always. Zazueta is coming over and . . . "

He gave me instructions, just like any other day. Then he got up from the table, went into the bathroom to finish getting ready, and gave me a good-bye peck on the cheek . . . as if nothing had happened.

Although it was painful, I refused to see Rodrigo for a week. That afternoon when he came to have his talk with Francisco, I called on a friend. During the next several days I refused to see him, because I knew that, once he turned on his charm, I would end up forgiving him.

But when I did see him I couldn't resist the temptation of asking how his meeting with his father had gone.

"No, mama, he wasn't angry, he didn't exactly scold me. It was ... how can I explain it ... sort of an analysis of my life with Isis ... a general meditation on work, on life ... but what made the biggest impact on me was a strange warning. I remember it perfectly: 'Happiness can be dangerous when carried to excess; once it ferments it makes things explode. And I'm not talking about passion, but about love carried to extremes aspiring to perfection. It may be unconscious and pure, but that's why it's so deceptive.'

That's what he told me."

I was concerned about the health of my son and daughter-in-law. He worked hard, really throwing himself into his job on the sugar plantation. The position had seemed too important for a twenty-four-year-old when he first came home from school, but within a year he had it completely mastered. He did it for my daughter-in-law's sake, since she didn't have any children and didn't seem to care. In her, the maternal instinct I thought was innate was definitely lacking.

They had gotten married as soon as he graduated; he was just twenty-three and she was nineteen. That was four years ago now. I was worried about Rodrigo's health, because, even working as hard as he did, a night didn't go by when he didn't stay up late entertaining guests at their house, or attending a dinner or dance at some friend's house, and he didn't get much sleep. In Isis's case, I wasn't exactly afraid she would get sick, since she had the easiest life in the world. Her household was run by Marta, a longtime servant, and Isis would sleep in, getting up just in time to get dressed and welcome Rodrigo home for the afternoon meal. That isn't what bothered me. What I wanted was grandchildren, lots of grandchildren, so I could take care of them and spoil them. I always regretted having had just one child. If only I had been given a daughter, too ... but the miscarriage ... no, it's better not to think about that.

That's why sweet tears wet my face that evening, when Rodrigo and Isis came over for dinner and we sat outside in the cool night air, with Isis playing those lovely nursery songs on Tita, her favorite guitar—those songs we had never heard her play before and that evoked Dutch linen, lemon trees in bloom, and the impulse to associate a baby with things of which it has no knowledge: the moon, horses, rivers, cradles, the sea, everything beautiful in the world, trees, birds. "So that it will feel at home here," she said, then fell silent, and for some reason we followed suit, enveloped in a tender silence interrupted only by the distant pounding of the sea.

Isis softly broke the silence: "What lovely stars there are tonight; I feel as if the little boy or girl I'm carrying in my womb is one of them."

And we could still hear the ocean when we, four happy beings, hugged each other with immense love, not daring to utter a word. Then, as soon as we could manage it, we said good-night, our eyes still moist.

The next day, bright and early, as soon as Francisco had driven away (they must have been spying on him from the corner), Petra and her daughters showed up.

"We're going to be grandparents, Isabelita! My daughters and I are so happy! I can just imagine how thrilled you and Francisco must be. We're going over to the sugar mill right now to buy some worsted and . . ."

As usual, she kept on talking nonstop. Before inviting them to sit down, I looked over Isis's sisters, Mercedes and La India, so like my daughter-in-law in every way: tall and self-assured, with a gracious, haughty pride. La India was light-complexioned, but not alabaster, like her sisters, including little Mina, although she was very blond and blue-eyed. Mina must have been about twelve then. As I watched her, she smiled sweetly. Seeing her like that, silent, innocent, as beautiful as her sisters, one would never guess she was mentally retarded. According to the doctors, she had the intelligence of an eight-year-old, but that wasn't the worst of it; I know a number of married women with children who are no more intelligent than that. Her misfortune was that she had tremendous difficulty speaking and she swallowed entire words, especially prepositions, so as soon as she opened her mouth, everyone realized she was abnormal. But she was the only one of the Astorga girls who knew how to iron, embroider, sew, cook, and keep house, all perfectly well. To make a long story short, she ran the household, because her sisters devoted themselves to their appearance and led very active social lives, since besides being beautiful (the different branches of the Astorga family are known throughout the state for their physical perfection), they are popular and vivacious. It seems like nothing can daunt them.

"... and when she's older, as I was saying, if it's a girl. You know that I'm happy not having sons, because men ..."

I had gestured for them to sit down and, now I interrupted Petra's monologue to ask the little one:

"Are you glad you're going to be an aunt?"

"Very—my baby—I going—give it bath—put on clothes."

"That's just fine. And you girls, what do you think?"

"I must confess I'm a little envious of Isis. I wish I were in her shoes," Mercedes said.

"Oh, no! What we have to do is get married right away so we won't have any reason to envy her," responded La India.

"Well, I'll be delighted to dance at your weddings. Out of all your suitors, who will the lucky ones be?"

"We haven't decided yet; we're waiting to fall in love, like Isis," said Mercedes.

"Well, she didn't have to wait long," I answered, smiling.

"No, they've been in love ever since they were little; I can remember."

Before she could go on reminiscing, I got up and said:

"You have a trip to the mill ahead of you, and I have plenty to do around the house. Why don't you let me know when it's convenient and, some evening when Francisco is home, we'll celebrate the good news with a dinner party." I stood up.

"I think that's a wonderful idea!" Mercedes said cheerfully.

"We'll bring the guitar and sing some songs."

Petra didn't look pleased, because around Francisco she had to talk as little as possible.

"Isis go? Odi go?" said Mina.

"Of course they'll be there; after all, they're the guests of honor," I replied.

I was concerned about that little girl's future; I loved her with all my heart. More than the others. Perhaps in order to compensate a bit for nature's injustice.

A few days later, I gave the dinner party: the family and a

few close friends. We drank, ate, played the guitar, and were very content well into the night.

Maybe that's what did it. I'd rather not even think that's what might have caused it, but the next morning Marta came running over, so out of breath she could barely speak.

"Miss Isis . . . Miss Isis . . ."

"What's wrong with Miss Isis?"

"She's bleeding and moaning."

Before summoning Francisco or Rodrigo, who I was told were in the fields, I called Dr. Izábal. Then I sent for the men and ran over to my children's house with Marta.

I got there and saw Isis lying in bed, moaning; I fearfully pulled back the sheet and saw two small bloodstains. She was clutching her stomach and moaning in a sort of childlike rhythm.

"Dr. Izábal is coming right away," I told her, "Don't worry, this will be over soon."

"My baby, my baby!" she whimpered softly, in pain.

I covered her up again and sat down at the head of the bed, wiping the sweat and tears from her face from time to time.

"Shhh, shhh, Darling, this will be over soon, it's nothing serious. . . . Relax, don't overdo it."

I don't know what all I said to calm her down, but I felt like someone had driven a stake into my heart.

The doctor made it from the mill where he lived to Rodrigo's house in fifteen minutes, at the most. An eternity. Marta showed him directly into the bedroom, and I stepped outside.

God only knows how much I suffered while Enrique was alone with Isis. I restlessly paced the hallway to calm myself down. I told Marta to have some lemon-grass tea made, a lot of it, for Isis and me. When she came back with the cup, my hands were trembling so that I couldn't drink it. What worried me the most was that Enrique Izábal was taking such a very long time in there. "I have to keep calm, I have to keep calm." I sat down in the drawing room, my back straight as a rod, my hands folded in my lap, and waited. The men still hadn't arrived.

I bounced up as if I were made of elastic when I saw the bedroom door open. I waited for him to speak.

Enrique came out haltingly, waving his right hand up and

down, in a gesture intended to soothe me. He walked over to me and asked:

"Can we talk alone?"

"Dear Lord! Let's go into the living room," I retorted.

We went in and I closed the door.

"Is it serious?"

"No, now don't get excited, Isabelita. Sit down and get ahold of yourself. Calm down, calm down . . . it hasn't detached itself; the fetus is still in place. But I questioned Isis closely and found out why she's bleeding. Today is precisely the day when her period should start. As you probably know, some women keep menstruating for a month or two, and others keep menstruating the whole nine months without any problem . . . the amount of blood she's lost is not significant, and we usually have the patient rest, just as a precaution, for one or two months, but in her case. . . . It's hard for me to say this." He cleared his throat and fell silent for a moment, then continued haltingly: "Look here, when I first arrived here, my first job was to bring Isis into the world. I've seen her through all her illnesses and I know her very well . . . she's a good girl . . . a darling girl . . . "

"Please go on, Enrique."

"Well, you know her, too. She's wild, immature; everyone pampers her—"

"Yes, I know all that; please, come right out and say what you've got on your mind."

"Fine; I've already told you that, if we were to keep an eye on her for another month or two, if she were to lead a quiet life, there surely wouldn't be any danger. But if we let her loose, she's liable to jump onto the first horse that comes by. I've told her she has to have complete bedrest up to the end of her pregnancy. I'm only confiding this in you and Francisco, since, if you'll forgive my saying so, your son can't control her . . . I—"

"You've said what you had to say and I thank you for it. I agree with you entirely, and Francisco will, too. You're a real doctor. Thanks again."

We said good-bye at the door, squeezing each other's hands like conspirators; then I set about calculating how I could keep Isis entertained during so many months in bed.

Francisco thought Izábal's decision and my plans very

reasonable: get-togethers every evening in Isis's bedroom, rearranging the furniture, bringing out Tita a lot, and having her sisters and friends keep her company, keeping her busy with knitting and needlework, putting a radio next to the bed, surprising her every so often with new nightgowns and robes, ordering the dishes she craved or even fixing them myself . . . in short, a complete plan, one we were not entirely sure of; but it worked. What bothered Isis the most was not being able to play the guitar for several months, because of her big belly. But I don't think she was so unhappy.

Francisco and I would go visit her every night, if only for a little while, since, if the truth were told, we were even more impatient than she was, and perhaps happier, expecting our grandchild.

It arrived at last. It was a little girl, and oh, *what* a little girl!

An Astorga. White as the purest marble, with big brown eyes, a perfect nose, and Isis's delicate lips, delicate and at the same time eager, just like her mother's.

She was born in our house, at Enrique's orders, so I could take care of mother and child. Although the birth was normal, Izábal found some excuse for Isis to keep the forty days' bedrest that new mothers used to observe. What a wise decision! Because afterward, when she was able to walk, she was the same as ever . . . no, worse.

I still remember very clearly seeing her, early one morning, still in her bathrobe, from the stand where I oversaw the sale of milk, cream, cheese, and so forth. She was absentmindedly watching the marvelous but unbroken mare's desperate prancing in the little corral. The mare was wearing only a halter and rope, because they hadn't managed to put even a bit on her. I felt afraid. I was holding the baby, whom she had nursed a little while earlier, when I had laid her down on Isis's breast, and the mother was sleeping so soundly that she barely noticed. I had chores to do around the house; I remember I wanted to make some cheese after balancing the books for the day. It was strange that she had gotten up early; maybe what woke her up was Francisco's announcement that he had bought a very fine mare that wasn't broken yet. That must have aroused her curiosity.

I held the baby and, with my free hand, picked up my papers. I circled the corrals, walked up to where she was standing, and invited her to come inside with me for breakfast.

"I'm not hungry yet," she told me, "I'll be in in a little while."

That frightened me even more and, as a security measure, I laid the baby in her arms, saying I had lots of chores to do.

I went into the house and began my usual routine.

When I heard someone shouting outside and realized it was coming from the corrals, my heart stopped.

I ran outside as fast as I could and headed straight for the little corral. Chico practically shouted at me:

"We had to open the gate for her. The mare was bucking so hard that we had to. And she's riding sidesaddle."

"What about the baby?" I yelled back.

"She took it with her, cradled in her left arm, hanging onto the saddlehorn with her right hand."

"Which way did she go?"

"She took off straight ahead; we couldn't make out where she turned off, if she did."

"My God!"

"I know, Doña Isabel. Four of us are saddling up to go track her down."

As if there would be tracks on those dusty roads!

I spoke to Francisco, Rodrigo. They couldn't believe it. At least I located them. I went to my room and kneeled down in the prie-dieu to pray, to pray with all my soul. With all my tears.

My husband and son arrived. I clung to Francisco, sobbing, and told him the little I knew. They, too, saddled their horses and rode off. They didn't even know where they were going. I was left alone with my tears and prayers.

An hour, two hours went by. . . . Dear Lord!

Suddenly, a big uproar in the corrals. I ran outside. Who was it? Who was it?

I saw Isis getting off the mare.

"Now she's broke," she said simply, with a pride she couldn't contain.

"And the baby?" I shouted desperately.

"I left her on the riverbank when the mare spooked."

I slapped her.

"Where did you leave her, damn you?"

She touched her hand to her cheek and stared at me, stunned.

"Out there, in the California meadows."

"Andrés, hitch up the big packsaddle for me, and hurry," I told the frightened boy.

Yes, I went to the meadow to find my little one. She was a tiny bundle of blankets and covers tossed next to the river bed . . .

At first she seemed to be sleeping, but no, she was unconscious and burning with fever.

Heartsick, I headed home. Francisco was waiting for me.

"Isabelita," he asked me, stifling a sob—. "Is she dead?"

"Not yet. Call the doctor, or better yet, let's drive her to the doctor in the car."

"Yes, let's hurry. Emilio!" he shouted. The chauffeur came and we took off. That motionless little body in my arms was barely breathing. Francisco asked to hold her, but I told him, "No, don't move her."

We finally arrived. When he saw our faces and the tiny baby in our arms, Enrique was stunned.

"What happened? I just saw her yesterday and—"

"There's no time for explanations," said Francisco. "Examine her. She's been lying on the sand, in the sun, for who knows how long."

No, I don't remember, I don't want to remember: her little back was an open wound, her tiny face full of blisters. And then, puncturing the skin of her little arm for the IV. . . . No crying. . . . She didn't cry.

Those were terrible days. I don't know what Rodrigo and Francisco did or said to Isis, but neither she nor her mother or sisters came near my room, where I watched over the baby day and night. I followed the instructions Izábal gave me to the letter; he paid her a visit every morning and afternoon.

Francisco and Rodrigo would help me, making me eat something and then rest until it was time to do something special for the infant. I wasn't hungry and couldn't sleep. My heart went out to my son, who would sit there, hovering over my bed, where she lay on her stomach, half-asleep, opening up the wounds on her cheeks every time she managed to squirm a little. Weeping, he would say to her with all the tenderness he could muster:

"My little one . . . my little one. . . . " And an eternity would go by.

Francisco took care of me; he made me eat, bathe, rest, and when he thought I was asleep in another room where he had laid me down, he would pace the long corridor, chain-smoking. Then he would go to our bedroom to keep Rodrigo company, but only from time to time. His impotence was killing him.

He told me that Rodrigo had had the locks of the house changed and had put the guitars under lock and key in his office. Isis was alone with Marta and the servants, crying. When they had to shop, he would unlock the door for Marta early in the morning and, as soon as she came back, he would lock them up again and go away. I was startled to learn that he was also sleeping, as much as he could, at our house, and not even Isis's pleading and tears could touch him. On the contrary, they made him all the more furious with her. In spite of what she had done, I pitied her; it was natural that she would want to see her daughter, see how she was doing, but for once Rodrigo was stern with her and Francisco didn't intervene. I think he was more wounded than his son.

The baby began to take some nourishment in the form of drops, but she still had the IV and hadn't opened her eyes. Still, she didn't cry, not even when I daubed the ointment on her wounds with a piece of organdy. Then she started to eat a little more, a little more . . . with an eyedropper. Until one afternoon she moaned and half-opened her swollen eyelids while Enrique was treating her.

"I think we're out of the woods," said Enrique, triumphant. Francisco and I hugged and kissed each other and also hugged Izábal.

"Take it easy, take it easy. The worst is over, but . . . " He gave new instructions and we continued nursing her back to health. I started dozing off now and then in the easy chair while I watched over her.

The weeks went by, slowly but no longer desperately. After four months the child's skin began to form; still, it was so tender that it couldn't be touched.

We would feed her with boiled milk from La Pinta, but she would hardly drink a drop.

The first day that she wailed with hunger, I called the men and the doctor to come see the miracle.

Cruelly, I let her cry for a while. Just for the pleasure of hearing her, and so I could ask Enrique for instructions on how to handle her now. I followed his advice and, at long last, she ate something.

When the three men arrived she was satisfied, sleeping peacefully.

"I'm not leaving here until she cries again," said Francisco.

"I'd even be willing to wake her up."

"I'm going to take the IV out. We'll have to sew up the vein. But we'll do it when she wakes up."

Oh, that open wound in her right arm!

"I'm not going to help you," I told him.

"I'll do it," murmured Rodrigo, lowering his eyes so we couldn't see his tears.

Francisco and I wordlessly went to the other hall so we couldn't hear the baby's cries. He told me that Rodrigo had been sleeping at his own house for two months now, but that Isis was still locked up.

Taking off their white robes, and Enrique his gloves, they came looking for us to tell us that the baby didn't seem to have suffered that much. Rodrigo suggested giving her a little tea and Enrique went off to the office with Francisco to write down the diet and care that the baby would require.

Afterward, Francisco offered us a drink, "to celebrate," and he had them bring cheese, olives, chorizo, everything there was in the house.

I got up my courage and said: "I think it's time that her mother saw her. That's the only thing missing in this celebration."

Izábal jumped:

"But Isis can't see her if she doesn't put on a white robe, and please don't let her touch the baby."

I laughed: "What about the baptism? I sprinkled her when we thought she was dying, but now we should make it official."

"In two or three months," said Enrique, "she should be able to face the long robe and the big hugs. . . . Let's say four."

"Her name will be Isabel. It's only right, Rodrigo, don't you think?"

If my poor son had other ideas, he kept them to himself and enthusiastically agreed.

We were so content . . . and then Francisco started singing:

"I don't cut cane anymore;
let the wind topple it;
let the women topple it
with their hips . . . "

"Francisco!"

He laughed heartily: "I did it to make you mad. You're so pretty when you're angry."

We all laughed and Rodrigo went to get Isis.

Our life slowly returned to normal and one day the little one went home. By now we called her La Tita, just like the guitar.

As a matter of fact, there was one time when Isis was careless again . . . but let's not talk about that anymore.

Despite her mother, Tita, the child, did survive. I have to admit that Isis kept her dressed up like a little princess. And every day her innocent beauty blossomed more and more.

Three years later, Isis got pregnant again. Our happiness was as great as it had been when we had been given the news that Tita was to be born.

But this pregnancy robbed us all of our happiness!

One morning, just like before, Marta came running into the house shouting.

"The mistress . . . the mistress is dying . . . "

I foolishly thought it was the same problem that had alarmed us once before. I called the doctor and, when I was on the verge of phoning Rodrigo and Francisco, Marta told me:

"Rodrigo is already with her . . . but hurry up, Isabelita, because . . . the mistress is dying . . . she's dying."

When I heard that, I put down the telephone and told Natalia to call Francisco.

And my God, what I encountered! Rodrigo sat at the head of the bed holding his wife, who was howling with pain.

Because Isis wasn't shouting; her voice barely paused to take in air. That steady scream tore her throat and penetrated our eardrums like arrows piercing our hearts. I tried to place a hot-water bottle on her stomach, and with one blow she knocked it off. No use. No use. That was the worst thing about that moment: there was nothing we could do.

Izábal arrived and examined her in our presence, because we refused to leave.

When he took off his gloves, I saw his grim face and then I knew.

"She wouldn't reach Culiacán alive," he said. "It's an ectopic pregnancy and she would need blood, an operation that she couldn't tolerate, much less after the rough journey and the hours we would lose. Her vital signs are already very weak."

Yes, that's what he told me, as we stood outside the room, but for some reason I remember it as if we had been standing inside.

My son was covering Isis's body with kisses, as if his lips could give her blood, warmth, warmth. A ghostly Isis was screaming softly, as in dreams, from the other side, that side that's unknown to us.

Rodrigo kept trying to bring her back to life with his kisses, holding her, telling her desperate words of love.

I kneeled on the other side of the bed and began to pray wordlessly.

Enrique was standing beside me, his hand on my shoulder.

When Francisco arrived, Isis was practically dead. Her wide-open eyes could no longer see; she couldn't hear; she no longer complained. Only a trace of air was entering her nostrils.

Pain, oh, such pain!

Enrique tried to determine if she was dead and then Rodrigo got up, furious, and told him:

"Don't you touch her. She's mine."

He took her in his arms as if to protect her from the whole world, and his wild eyes glared at us hatefully.

We had to give him a shot in the arm, through his shirt, to make him lose consciousness and finally let go of her. Those were unspeakable hours that I'd rather not remember.

Chico and Pablo took Rodrigo to our house in the car,

driven by Emilio. We held the wake and buried Isis. Enrique stayed with Rodrigo.

For many days and nights Rodrigo was wracked by delirium, fever, and cold; he wouldn't eat a bite or take a drink.

Then he fell into a horrible depression.

We reached an agreement with Enrique to send him far away, very far away. We made up the story that he was going away to study sugar mills and we sent him off, sedated, to the United States. First to a nursing home and then to forget.

Chico and Pablo were retainers, houseservants in the Spanish sense: they had grown up with us and were part of the family.

Chico's letters, while Rodrigo was in the nursing home, naturally included the medical reports, but they were written above all to entertain us, to soothe our nerves, telling us all about his own adventures and linguistic defeats; since he didn't speak English, he didn't even know where the buses he got on were going, or what he was eating. The letters achieved their purpose. Then he started sending us brief messages from Rodrigo, written coherently but with an unsteady hand. At the end of six months, Rodrigo was released; he still had to take some medication, but in the company of Chico, who had mastered broken English, he traveled around the United States.

A year later we received a long letter from Rodrigo in which he told us that his salvation had been taking a vital interest in something, that, to prepare for his career and his work here, he needed to get a master's in industrial chemistry.

We wanted to see him. After what had happened, after the condition we had last seen him in, we *needed* to see him, but . . . we agreed, feigning enthusiasm. We asked him to send us photographs and he did: he had changed; he looked older, wore a mustache now and a serious expression had transformed him. But as for his looks, he was handsomer than ever; like Natalia said, more *interesting*. Chico came back speaking almost perfect English.

Tita was growing up. Between Francisco and I, we spoiled her rotten. She was a very pampered child and so she was very headstrong, but she had her mother's grace and her father's charm, and we couldn't resist letting her have her way. She was the apple of our eyes.

From the time she was little she was a flirt and had a strong personality. For example, she had to choose the clothes she would wear, and she went wild over the tiny pieces of jewelry that we had made for her. To go with each dress, shoes, and stockings, she would have us put this or that ornament in her beautiful, wavy chestnut hair, just like her mother's; she would wear this little bracelet or that little ring. She knew perfectly well what clothing became her. The same thing with her hair. Oh, how I enjoyed dressing her!

During Rodrigo's absence, Mercedes and La India both found love and married "very well," as Petra would say. The former to a businessman from Los Mochis and the latter to a doctor who set up practice in Guadalajara. So Petra was left all alone with Mina, who was now sixteen, so lovely and so unfortunate. But for her everything was a cause for joy, even the most insignificant things: she was a child.

Rodrigo announced he was coming home. We rearranged the furniture in his house; we had the house painted inside and out. I worked hard on the houseplants and in the garden, and we awaited him impatiently.

When we went to meet him in Culiacán, Francisco and I barely spoke, either on the road or in the waiting room. We were afraid of betraying our excitement to each other. But when we saw him coming down the ramp, our eyes filled with tears. Still, we embraced him dry-eyed, as if he had been away only for a few weeks. The photos had been accurate; he came back changed, but for the better; at least, that's what we thought.

When he got home, he immediately noticed the pains we took to please him. He looked at us and smiled, hugging us both.

We threw a big party, for his friends and ours, which means we invited practically the whole town. We slaughtered a pig and barbecued a steer. We shut up the ornery geese; anyway, six of them were ready for the table. There was music and plenty of food.

In spite of it all, my heart was not at peace: Tita, who was now seven, had always refused to listen to or read the letters that her father Rodrigo sent her. She barely looked at the photos. She adamantly refused to go with us to meet him in Culiacán, and now I had to look for her all over the house. I found her in the feeding troughs, somewhere she never went. There she was, so serious, as impeccably dressed as I had left her, sitting on the step and listening to the distant sound of music and murmur of voices.

"What are you doing here? Go say hello to your daddy."

"He isn't my daddy."

"Of course he is, and don't act silly because I'll get mad and you know what happens when I get mad."

She got up, scowling, and took my hand. We went to Rodrigo's bedroom, where I had told him to wait.

When we walked in he immediately lifted her up by the waist, overcome with happiness and excitement and, holding her up to his face, he twirled her around and around, saying in a voice choked with emotion, "My baby, my baby. . . . " Then he pressed her to his chest and kissed her little face, her hands, her arms. Still very serious, she let him do it, and when he asked her for a kiss, she coolly gave it to him and said: "Let me down."

He complied and stood there looking at her. A cloud of sadness darkened his features for a moment, but, sweeping his hands over his eyes as if to wipe it away, he started talking to her:

"I couldn't wait to see you. You don't remember me because you were very little. Now we're going to always be together and we'll have a great time, won't we? I brought you a lot of presents. Do you want to see them?"

She was silent.

"You know I'm your daddy, don't you?"

"My daddy's name is Francisco."

"That's right, but I'm your daddy too, your daddy Rodrigo. You're lucky; you've got two daddies."

"I've only got one," she said, and turning around, she walked stiffly out of the room.

He was bewildered, saddened, kneeling there on the floor with his arms still open wide.

I tried to comfort him: "She'll get over it. Little by little she'll get used to your being around." And then, laughing: "You can't have two daddies at once."

"But . . . "

"Never mind, never mind. Let's go to the party. This other business will gradually work itself out."

Rodrigo thoroughly enjoyed his homecoming. He even sang along to the guitar music. Tita watched him warily from a corner. In private Francisco and I embraced, overjoyed at having recovered the son who had left us in such a state and had come back completely cured.

It was soon apparent that Rodrigo's studies were relevant and bore fruit. Scarcely two years went by before they named him general manager. Because of that, he said that he needed his own house (which the company would give him) and I think he needed more than ever to avoid the slights of little Tita, who reminded him of Isis and kept openly rejecting him. Also, rumor had it that he wanted to get married again, possibly to Enrique Izábal's youngest daughter, Laura, or to Delia Ibarra, or to . . . how would I know; there were flirtations, gossip . . . but he definitely had an active social life and the girls found him very attractive, because of both his personality and his position.

Marta kept house for him again and Mina would go over, after dinner, to iron his clothes. (Linen is hard to iron and he was arrogant enough to ask her to do it for him.)

Francisco and I wished with all our hearts that Tita would learn to love her father, but she reacted to our overtures by drawing even closer to Francisco. She had him teach her to play dominoes and chess so they could spend time together in the evening. At the tender age of nine or ten she was already an expert. She was affectionate with me and liked to entertain me by singing while I sewed or darned. She was a princess, like her mother.

One day, Petra came to call; she was uncharacteristically silent and reserved. After a lot of beating around the bush, she blurted it out:

"Mina's pregnant."

I was speechless. Then I became furious:

"What animal could have done that to her?"

"I don't know. When I question her about him, she will only say, 'pretty,' 'handsome,' but I haven't been able to get the name out of her, even when I beat her with a stick."

"You shouldn't do that! Don't *you* act like a monster, too! She's a victim. Don't you understand?"

"Victim! Victim! She's a slut, a whor—"

"Don't say that! That just isn't true! And now I think you'd better leave."

Fortunately, Rodrigo came home right after she had left. Luckily, Francisco wasn't there. In Rodrigo's presence, all my indignation, all my pain, exploded. I vented it all in word and gesture, without even looking at him.

When I turned around, he had turned as pale as a corpse, hanging his head and clutching his hat in his hands. With great difficulty he began to speak:

"That horrid man is me, Mother."

I couldn't even respond.

"Please, listen to what I have to say as if this were a confession, with no interruptions."

I was sleeping in my underwear, with all the doors and windows shut, so the room was dark, when I heard a noise and half-opened my eyes. I saw Isis bent over, putting something in the dresser. Without thinking, I jumped up and grabbed her by the waist; she bent over further and I started kissing the nape of her neck, her shoulders, and, with my eyes closed, I turned her around and kissed her on the mouth. She kept still and, after a moment, returned my kisses, in that special way of hers. I took her in my arms and lay her down on the bed: the same skin, the same body . . . yes, I took her clothes off and glimpsed her adolescent body, like those first times; I caressed her, I loved her with all my heart . . . and only when I came to did I realize that it hadn't been a dream. Mina was asleep at my side . . . If you feel horrified now, just imagine what it was like for me to come out of that dream, and discover that . . . only the color of her hair told me that she wasn't the woman I loved . . . she moaned the same way, she moved the same way . . . and now . . . I was a bastard for having loved her. I was terrified. I hurriedly got dressed, yes, like a coward, and I ran away before Mina could open her innocent, blue eyes . . .

But *that* was a dream, not an evil act. The evil came later, the next day, when I opened my eyes and saw Mina standing next to me, naked, with the same body, the same face as Isis's, and the white gold of her hair falling down to her waist.

"Play?" she said to me.

"Yes, but don't talk, don't say a word. Shhhh."

Then I did make love to Isis with the troubled realization that it wasn't she, but another woman who was almost she . . . I can't explain it.

I'm a bastard. I know. But having even a part of Isis gave me more happiness than anything else in the world. I was horribly selfish; I never thought about Mina, about Mina the person, only about the other woman. And now . . .

He was running his fingers through his hair, hanging his head.

After a long pause he stood up and said firmly: "I'll marry her."

I couldn't speak. I got up and walked to my room like a zombie. To try and understand.

Yes, in simple terms, the truth was brutal, despicable, vile in every sense, but deep down, very deep down, it was an act of love that reproduced, intact, other acts of love, acts deeply desired, dreamed of . . . "one more time," "just one more time," he must have hoped so often, and a miracle, this fervent dream, had come true. Sin came afterward, when the miracle had stopped being a miracle and he had abused it by forcing it to repeat itself. Excess, always excess. And now . . . what should be done? The Erinia women were beginning to torment my son and he was willing to turn himself over to them. Would it be wise to stop him?

The worst thing about his marrying Mina was that he didn't love her. He was merely searching in her for a reflection of the other woman. And as for communication, how could he communicate with her, comment on his work and his thoughts and feelings? Also, he would have to play the role of a bachelor in society, while Mina would serve as his housekeeper and the object of a desire that might suddenly disappear, once she was no longer a mystery, a miracle. And the baby? Would it have to be a child they got "somewhere"? Not almost Isis's baby? My God, forgive him . . . forgive him and, in your divine wisdom, find a solution to this problem.

Francisco and I talked the situation over at length. He was openly opposed to a wedding, although he had some doubts.

"The baby can live perfectly well with Mina, at Petra's house, with all the care and comfort it's within our power to give them. Petra would miss Mina, and she adores money. She'll agree. Rodrigo will recognize his child legally; he can see to its education and socially . . . you know how people are. After the scandal has subsided, they'll be better off getting along with the manager than closing their doors to him or withdrawing their friendship."

"And what about Mina? She's in love with him. . . . Why should she be the one to pay?"

"Someone has to come out the loser. Don't worry; she'll forget him. She'll see as little of Rodrigo as possible. She'll forget, like all children do."

"Look at me. Do you really believe that?"

"No. But there isn't any other way out."

Dear God, show us the way! Offer us a solution that won't be cruel to any of them, including the child! Help us in our hour of need!

And God heard me, but what a cruel response he gave! Rodrigo was killed in a horrible, inexplicable car accident. In the marshes, when he slammed on the brakes and the car rolled over. What could have run out in from of him? What on earth was he doing there? Why was he driving so fast? In those marshes that are nothing more than a hard, sandy crust left by the sea, desolate, their only attraction solitude. What was my son looking for? Solitude? And why in his car, driving like a bat out of hell and. . . . What could have crossed his path to make him slam on the brakes and flip the car over? There isn't anything out there. Dear Lord! Spare me the horrible temptation of thinking it was suicide!

I begged Francisco to let me wash Rodrigo's wounds, however dreadful, with my own hands. To dress him like I used to when he was a child. Francisco wouldn't allow it.

"You have to understand that he's horribly disfigured. You wouldn't even recognize him."

Oh God! All powerful God! What have you done? What have you done to us all?

Shadows, we have lived like shadows ever since.

The blackness covered everything, leaving not a point of light to look at, not a gust of wind to breathe. Everything lost its meaning; there is no name to call us: neither orphans, nor widows . . . there is no name to call those of us who have lost a child, because we no longer live, although we might exist. And that cruel thought in the depths of one's soul. Francisco had it too. I'm sure of it. On his grim forehead, in his clenched mouth there was the same thought. No one breathed a word about the circumstances of the *accident*.

After the funeral the door of the house stood closed, in this town full of open doors, and no one dared call on us.

Until we heard loud knocking early one morning: it was La India and Mercedes, telling us that Mina was going into hard labor. The whole household was set in motion and, at that instant, Francisco said some things that might have passed for nonsense:

"I believe that, in some cases, he who takes justice into his own hands is courageous."

After taking every precaution, we went to Petra's house.

Mina's daughter was finally born. The birth was normal, but Mina cried out and wept without grasping what was happening to her.

"She's perfectly healthy. She's normal, and lovely. I hadn't seen such a beautiful baby since the birth of . . . "

Tita. That's what he meant. We went in to see her and were astonished; she was identical to Tita, although as time went by it became apparent that she had inherited her mother's blue eyes and blond coloring: another Astorga. Another granddaughter, even less fortunate than the first.

Tita was very pleased by Lila's birth. Just like Mina, when she came into the world, Tita wanted to bathe her and dress her from the beginning. But when she saw her for the first time, she was surprised that she could be so tiny, and when I placed the baby in Tita's arms, she said, alarmed: "Take her away! Take her away! I'm going to drop her!"

She was only able to enjoy her "little cousin" at her Grandma Petra's house, and for just a few months, since she was going away to a boarding school i Culiacán. It wasn't possible for her to come home every weekend, since at that time the famous highway wasn't what it is today; then it was no more than a dirt road, and during the rainy season the mud made it nearly impassable.

Tita was leaving . . . now we would have Lila, and only now and then. And Tita's vacations, her eagerly anticipated vacations.

Petra died and, naturally, Mina and Lila came to live with us.

Lila called Francisco Daddy, and one summer afternoon, when she was two years old and was walking toward his out-stretched arms, in a fit of jealousy Tita placed herself between them and told the baby, "He isn't your daddy! He isn't your daddy!"

Lila looked at her in astonishment, and when she saw Tita's fierce expression, she started to cry. I immediately took her into my arms and sat her down in Francisco's lap.

"He is too her daddy! As much her daddy as yours!"

Tita retorted angrily:

"She has her mommy, Mina. I've got you. She must have a daddy, like me; they say I used to have one, but the only daddy I've got is Papa Francisco. Let her call her own father Daddy."

"She doesn't have a daddy, except Papa Francisco, because her own daddy died."

"Like mine?"

"Just like yours."

I couldn't bear that painful dialogue anymore. Telling the truth, but lying. Remembering my son and. . . . I went to my room, carrying Lila in my arms. I lay her on my bed and sat down next to her. "My baby, my baby," I said to her through my kisses and tears, and I observed her beauty, shining all the more brightly in the sunlight streaming into the room.

When I went back, to struggle with my conscience once again, Tita was sitting in Francisco's lap and caressing him. My husband was taken with that enchanting creature; I put Lila on his other knee and Tita got furious again; she climbed down from the armchair and went out into the vestibule. I could hear her slam-ming doors all the way through the house. She was beside herself with anger; I knew her. Francisco took Lila in his arms and assured me:

"She'll get over it; it's just a tantrum. Anyway, she's always loved Lila."

"She's never been jealous of anyone, because we taught her that you were the center of the universe and your center was her."

"No, Isabelita, you'll see . . . "

But no, that vacation went by, followed by another and another, and Tita's jealousy increased, instead of decreasing, al-though she did learn how to control it, at least in our presence.

But when they were alone together, I would spy on them, and I heard Tita sing Lila songs (Tita taught herself to play the guitar) from another time, songs her aunts had taught her. It seemed to me like it was Isis singing to her.

But as for her daddy, no one had better touch him in front of her. My warnings, my threats (which she knew to be idle) were useless. So were Francisco's.

So we decided to avoid unpleasantness and, during summer vacations, we would send Lila and Mina to Guadalajara or Los Mochis, to stay with Mercedes or La India, who were delighted to have them, since Mina would take charge of the house and they could take it easy.

Lila was eight years old when Tita decided to get married, to a Oaxacan she had fallen for. Yes, he was handsome, charming, generous with gifts; he barely drank, smoked very little, and owned good farmlands down south.

We sent Pablo incognito to ask around in Oaxaca, and it turned out that what Raúl had told us was an understatement. Handsome, from a good family, wealthy, gallant, and generous. What could we tell the girl? That it would hurt us if she went so far away? Was that any reason to object? Of course not. So we gave our consent and Raúl's parents came to ask for Tita's hand.

We agreed that the wedding would be in November, when the weather here is splendid. And we started working, ordering things, importing things. After all, we wanted the bridal trousseau to be the best that money could buy.

The problem came up when we were planning the wedding procession. Tita wanted six of her friends from boarding school for bridesmaids, and there were no objections. The objection came when Francisco, who knows so little about such things, had an idea:

"Why don't we have Lila walk in front of everybody, carrying a little basket of flowers."

Feeling pleased with himself, he didn't realize how angry his idea made Tita until he heard her scream:

"Lila is not going to lead my wedding procession! Do you understand? She's not going to lead my wedding procession!"

We were all dumbfounded at such a violent explosion over such a trivial matter. Was it caused by hatred for Lila? Perhaps envy? But why? Because she was blond? Because she was a child? Because they were putting her in front?

Silence. Then Francisco stood up and said: "We'll talk about it some other time."

Days of few words: "Good morning," "Good-night," and silence at the table. Little Lila, who had not been present at the scene over the procession, didn't understand what was going on. She would speak and we would barely respond, politely, it's true, but only the bare minimum. Observing such pettiness in Tita had us paralyzed. We just couldn't understand it.

Until one afternoon, when Francisco had just gotten home and was reading the newspaper and I was sitting next to him, sewing, Tita came walking toward us, her hair disheveled and her face swollen from crying. She got down on her hands and knees before us and, with her forehead touching the floor, said:

"Forgive me, Mama! Forgive me, Daddy! I'm wicked."

And her body was wracked by uncontrollable sobs.

"All my life I've been wicked. No, at first I wasn't, but when I started growing up . . . I'm sorry, I'm sorry!"

I kneeled down beside her to console her, and Francisco followed suit. She was having a real attack of hysterics. I went to get the sherry, had them make lemon-grass tea, brought smelling salts. Finally, exhausted, she let herself be carried to an armchair.

"I'm just like him . . . just like him . . . wicked. How could he have? . . . and I finished the job, thinking only about myself . . . and she's innocent . . . and Mina is innocent . . . and me, I'm a snake in the grass."

"No, dear, don't say things like that. Who was it that told you that story?"

"My Aunt Natalia."

My sister, that spiteful woman, had wanted to drive a stake into the tenderest flesh, into the one we loved the most, but she had done us a great favor by opening up the sore that had caused us so much suffering.

This story is the bitter soil on which our grandchildren are happily being born and raised, and on which our lovely Lila blossoms.

On Love

For Jorge de la Luz

Great lovers don't have any children. Neither the fair-skinned Isolde nor Isolde with the golden locks bore Tristan's children; Nefertiti didn't give Akhenaton any offspring. Passion that consumes everything doesn't obey the laws of Nature but rather those of the Spirit.

Rachel unwittingly obeyed this rule and, although Jacob made love to her every night, she was sterile. On the other hand, Leah, the cross-eyed usurper, conceived with every halfhearted encounter that religious duty required of her husband. But Rachel watched her husband's flocks grow, and watched Leah's youngsters learning to give the shepherds orders, getting lost in distant lands, searching for grass for their sheep, and returning contented, to whisper about their discoveries in their father's ear. He would smile and caress them lovingly.

Rachel was unfaithful to her love when she allowed herself to feel envy, when she renounced her role as the One True Love for the sake of having Jacob's paternal love. So she could sow and harvest like any other woman, when her destiny was not work but pleasure. And, for one whole night, she sold the pleasure reserved for her alone; she sold it to Leah in exchange for a fertility potion, and she gave birth, with unspeakable pain, to that child who grew up to be one of the most beautiful men humanity had ever known. She achieved what she wanted: the perfect work of art, deserving of his father's love. But she didn't live to see it, because while giving birth to Benjamin, who would consolidate her triumph, she died. The father hated the innocent assassin and Rachel didn't live to witness Jacob's excessive love for Joseph. Her victory was hollow: Joseph became an Egyptian and no one acknowledged Benjamin's tribe. On the other hand, Leah's children, despite their sins, are kings and priests with the countless offspring that Jehovah promised to Jacob. But Jacob died in desolation. The Spirit had taken its revenge.

Old stories and wise tales: Theodore, the young poet, knew them all and would smile with satisfaction, because he and Myriam had been ideal lovers since adolescence, and people were amazed that their passion could last so many years without diminishing.

Myriam was radiant as the sun; she didn't wear any adornments and, nevertheless, her slender body, her long hair, her eyes, and her haughtiness stopped traffic and halted conversations. Still, she labored at difficult tasks in wealthy homes. The home of a poet is both luxury and poverty.

It was a luxury for Theodore to gather his friends every night at his house, with plenty of dates, olives, and fragrant, robust wine. First one would read, then another would read, the poems would change hands; they would laugh, debate, fall silent. Then Myriam would pick up the psaltery and her music would penetrate everyone's soul. She would sing Theodore's poems with such delicacy and feeling that words and music were one and the same thing. She didn't express opinions when the men debated, but with zither and voice would pass judgment on the best poems of their friends.

Later, in bed she would dangle her curls in Theodore's face and softly, very softly, conjure up with her musical voice the poems he had composed so long ago that he had all but forgotten them; they would come back to life and run through the young man's veins like some elegantly alien substance. Theodore would silence her with his mouth and press himself against her, knowing she held within herself all of him and more: the part that shimmered from ancient songs, from other epochs and other lands, distant lands, and—especially—she herself, an enigma he found disconcerting at times. He would search desperately for the secret in her body, but he never found the key to her perfection, not even by pleasuring her until she screamed.

When, without breaking her steady rhythm, Myriam would catch him watching her do chores, she would cast him a sidelong glance and smile maliciously.

But she committed the same sin as Rachel: she asked him for a child. He grew gloomy. He couldn't explain to her that it was only the Spirit that prevented it. She begged him, promising that the baby would be so good it would never cry, that it would be lulled to sleep by poems, words, and music, that everything would be just the same as ever. She didn't realize that Nature would come in, shattering the absolute. He closed himself off and suffered so much that his flesh shriveled and poetry tossed him aside like an old rag, and he knew neither thirst, hunger, sleep, nor friends: she had not understood. Then, without a word, he went away.

He walked the desert with his bare feet over the burning sand, his clothes in tatters, never finding the horizon. He lost himself and could find no repose.

Until one day, half-dead, lacking the strength to open his eyes, he realized that his head was resting in a woman's lap. He lost consciousness and when he finally came to in bed, an unbearable pain filled his being, but he could remember nothing.

He lived gratefully with that faceless woman. She bore him children that Theodore barely noticed. Leah, that pathetic name.

He abandoned that woman who had unwittingly saved his life. Perhaps there was another woman like her. What we know for sure is that there were many who, out of love, fed him and shared his bed, and he never knew their names; he couldn't even remember to call them by name.

But none of that mattered to him, nor did the hard labor he performed in other people's fields.

Until one day, when he cut a bunch of grapes, the sun

sparkled in one of them, in just one of the grapes in the bunch. The Spirit had returned and he recognized it.

As the years went by, he became the greatest poet of his time. Young people would come to him to learn all the forms, the rhythms, the secrets of technique. But while they drank fragrant wine and ate black olives, they would still recite the verses of his youth, and he would close his eyes and hear the zither and the voice singing. Though he refused to admit it, those poems were his masterpiece, and what breathed life into them was a god like Athon, a son like Joseph, a death for the sake of love.

Old now, he sits on a rock clutching the verses he has been writing since his resurrection, under the Spirit's mantle, until he has finally achieved perfection; he crumples the sheets penned by his hand and flings them into the sea. Not a single one of them is the poem of Nature and the Spirit. Deep down he could never tame Nature in his soul, try as he might, and now he is utterly alone, because those who heard Myriam's tale and understood the cause of his misery, crying their eyes out and tearing their breasts, can no longer mourn his second death, since all of them are dead.

Shadow in the Shadows

For Conchita Torre

Before I met Samuel I was an innocent woman . . . but pure? I don't know. I haven't thought about it that much. Perhaps if I had been, that crazy passion for Samuel wouldn't have welled up inside me—for Samuel, who will die only when I die. It may also be that, precisely through that passion, I have been purified. If he came and awakened the demon we all harbor within us, it isn't his fault.

From the broken window in the servants' quarters, where no one has lived for so long now, I watch a town I don't recognize go by. I don't know the newcomers, and the faces of the children I used to play with have grown hardened and old; I couldn't reconstruct them. But *they* know who I am and that's why they treat me the way they do if I try to venture out, even to buy an onion, in order to smell like the street, like open air again. In here everything is shut up and caged, as if the treasures this house once contained still existed! One of them is me.

When I turned fifteen Ermilo Paredes was forty-seven.

That's when he began to court me, but, of course, the one he really courted was my mother.

Through flattery, splendid afternoons in the country, gifts of grain, fruit, meat, canned goods, and even a priceless jewel on my birthday, little by little he broke down my mother's resistance so he could marry me. He was reputed to be a depraved lecher.

"No, Doña Asunción, you pay no attention to that jealous gossip. I'll treat your daughter like a princess and keep her every bit as pure as she is now. But in a different social and moral universe, of course. I've been around, but I know how to value purity of the soul and to respect it. And why have I chosen Laura? No doubt for her natural gifts and striking beauty, but also because her mother is such a virtuous woman, who must have provided a magnificent example for her. You'll see, your daughter won't be stained by even an evil thought."

My mother hesitated between the neighbor ladies' advice and her own need for power and wealth. When she asked me about whether I wanted to marry him, I was indifferent, but when she described the wedding dress, the new house and many servants that would be mine, I thought how much I hated housework and about the prospect of marrying a man as poor as us, who would burden me with children, dirty plates, and dirty laundry; so I decided to get married. I had no feelings for Ermilo one way or the other. He was a close friend of Mama's. And that meant he must be a good man.

My engagement ring caused a stir among my girlfriends.

From the kitchen, I had heard Ermilo tell Mama: "You give it to her; I'm afraid my touch and the gift itself might frighten her." My friends said: "Oh yes, do get married!" "Just imagine how many dresses you could buy with this one gift"; ". . . and he isn't such an ugly fellow; old, but not ugly"; ". . . and he's such a gentleman"; "How thoughtful of him not to give it to you personally so he doesn't have to touch you."

Everything smiled on my engagement except for Ermilo's tedious visits. He talked to Mama about crops, old gossip, his relatives, and especially his properties and well-stocked grocery store. He kept Mama up-to-date on its sales record and prices, though she never had to set foot in it herself, since every morning he sent her a big basket overflowing with dry goods.

The ripple of silk and organdy, linen and muslin, wool,

velvet, drove me wild; trying on clothes; admiring myself in the mirror; opening boxes from Paris—these things had me beside myself, and I would dwell on and relish them, eating bonbons while Ermilo and Mama chatted.

I wanted Mama to come live with us but, smiling coquettishly, she repeated the famous dictum, "For each married man, a house to himself," and Ermilo pretended he hadn't heard a word. The one thing I asked for was denied me.

My wedding dress was the most elegant the town had ever seen. The solemn ceremony was performed by the bishop himself. Afterward there was a sumptuous banquet in the park behind the house with its firs and birch trees. In the garden across the street, food was served and alms were given to the poor, so they would pray for our happiness.

As evening fell, my mother and Ermilo grew more and more fidgety. I couldn't understand why. Perhaps because that hectic day was coming to an end as the guests left.

My mother dragged me behind some bushes.

"Are you scared?" she asked me.

"Scared of what?"

She seemed very disturbed. At last she said: "Of being alone with Ermilo."

"Why should I be? He'll lead the conversation and I'll follow."

"Even if it isn't a conversation, you just follow him." My mother's tone of voice was fearful, and she suddenly pressed me to her chest and began to sob. "I should have talked to you earlier ... but I couldn't.... Tonight mysterious things will happen and you'll have to be brave." My mother sobbed a little more, then she collected herself and said good-bye to Ermilo. She was the last to leave.

Those broken words of my mother's didn't make me afraid, but curious, and a little flame of hope began to flicker inside me. If there was something mysterious in that house, my relationship with Ermilo might not be so boring.

At bedtime that night, Ermilo asked me if I knew we were going to sleep together. No, I didn't know. Then he took me by the hand, and holding both of our hands up high, as if we were dancing, we went upstairs to the second floor. "No one but us sleeps in this wing of the house," he said, and opened a big door. Never in my wildest dreams had I imagined a bedroom so enormous, so sumptuous, so stuffed with furniture and heavy drapes. The bed was huge and the comforter was pulled down to the footboard.

"This is your room. Mine is next door," he said. I instinctively plopped down on the bed to test the mattress; it was made of goose feathers, and the canopy cast Chinese shadows in the candlelight as I jumped up and down on it in my bare feet.

"Don't do that!" shouted Ermilo, in a thunderous voice I had never heard before. I was petrified. I humbly climbed down onto the rug and waited, in my wedding dress, for the following orders.

"Now you'll go to your dressing room, which is off to the right, and get undressed. After you're naked you'll lie down in bed and wait for me. But don't dally."

Naked! My mother certainly should have talked to me before. Overcome with shame, I removed my jewelry and slipped off the dress with its thousand hooks. Once I had nothing on, I kicked the clothes lying at my feet. But my fury was extinguished by my fear of what might happen next. Of what *would* happen whether I liked it or not.

Hanging my head, I left the dressing room. I lay down in bed as I had been told and, pretending to be asleep, I kept perfectly still, my back glued to that mattress that had seemed so fantastic. When I could bear it no longer, I pulled the sheet up over my face. I squeezed my eyes shut.

I didn't have long to wait. The sheet was lowered very slowly and I felt fresh, fragrant buds begin to brush my hair, my face: lemon blossoms. The sheet kept coming down until my whole body was covered with those flowers. A sweet drunkenness spread over my arms and legs. Ermilo started kissing the flowers, one by one, but his lips didn't touch my skin. Enveloped by that heady perfume, I let him kiss the open lemon blossoms and, like them, I began to open up. I felt something caressing my insides with the tenderness one uses to pick lemon blossoms. There were no kisses or embraces, and I scarcely felt his body brushing against mine. Rather, I would say that a shadow possessed me, for the sake of my own pleasure, for my private delight. In the aftermath of my delicious, slow spasm, I drifted off to sleep amid the flowers, and no one disturbed my sleep.

I woke up lazily, entirely covered and surrounded by the dying fragrance of the fruit of the regal lemon trees. Those waxy, silken buds, like me, were at the height of their glory.

Ermilo peered in at the door, as he must have done many times that morning, since the sun was now high in the sky, and I called out to him in a deep, unfamiliar voice.

"Ermilo, I feel so happy. But come take these flowers away now; they make me feel like I'm wearing a shroud."

"You are wearing a shroud now," he responded, and sought my mouth anxiously, but I turned away; I had never been kissed, by him or anyone else. He tried to throw himself on top of me, but a wave of repulsion made me sit up and retch until he let go of me.

"One day at a time," he said. "Put on a robe and I'll send for your breakfast."

My mother must have been spying on the house for hours, because as soon as Ermilo had left she began ringing the doorbell furiously. I heard her come bounding up the stairs, and when I calculated that her round face was about to appear in the crack of the door, I loudly threw the bolt. She must have been stunned, but her guilt prevented her from pounding on the door as she would have done otherwise.

I deliberately walked into what, from that day on, would be my sitting room, adjoining the bedroom. I carefully shut the door between the two rooms and opened the hall door. My mother was still standing where she had been when I had slammed the door in her face. Then she saw me and practically pounced on me:

"What happened?"

"He wanted to kiss me but I wouldn't let him."

"You didn't let him? Then I guess . . . "

"Breakfast is served, Mother. Would you like to join me for breakfast?"

"Yes, of course, but what about last night . . . "

"Taste a croissant; they're hot and flaky."

"But darling . . . "

"Excuse me, but I have a lot to do."

"To do?"

"I have to take a bath and get dressed. Do you think that's not important? It's getting really late. Now I *must* look like a lady. Don't you agree?"

A dark resentment made me wish my mother would leave right away; I wasn't sure exactly why.

Eloísa was awaiting me with a delightful, lukewarm bath.

I took a long time deciding what dress and jewels to put on. Eloísa fixed my hair in an entirely new style: combed straight in front, with curls piled up in back. My dress was floor-length and that bothered me. I was used to wearing an ankle-length skirt, over white stockings and flats; now I *had* to wear heels.

"La Señora looks lovely, lovely," Eloísa exclaimed, pressing her hands together in admiration.

"Thanks to you, Eloísa. But I don't know what to do with this skirt and shoes."

"Take my hand and let's walk around the room. That way you'll start getting used to them, little by little."

We had a good laugh at my stumbling attempts to be graceful. And she had just helped me descend the stairs, to a luminous drawing room on the ground floor, when they announced that Lidia and Ester were here to see me. All I wanted to do was show off my finery. My finest clothes? No, I had quite a selection, so I wouldn't say that outfit was the most elegant. It was just an ordinary dress.

When they saw me walk in on Eloísa's arm, their mouths fell open. But when Eloísa left and I tried to walk over to them, I fell flat on the floor. All three of us burst out laughing, and we were once again the close friends we had always been.

Time flew by as we remarked on the events of the previous day; that so-and-so had this . . . and so-and-so had that . . . and oh! the sherbets and cake . . . we were still greedily remembering them when someone knocked at the door. I asked Ester to open it; I wasn't sure how to get up in my new outfit. It was Simón, the butler, asking if we wanted some refreshments. I told him deliberately, "Of course." A little while later, Simón himself came in, along with two maids, carrying cold drinks and all sorts of sweets. While they were serving us, I gave my first order as lady of the house.

"Simón, I want there to always be plenty of these things in the house."

"As you wish, Señora."

"And tomorrow I want sherbets, just like today."

"You need say no more."

As soon as they left, my two girlfriends flung themselves down on the floor, doubled over in laughter. "You did a terrific job . . . you were splendid."

When the commotion was over, we dedicated ourselves to enjoying all those delicacies: candied walnuts, all kinds of little cakes, pastas, bonbons, candies; in short, everything under the sun or even imaginable, since, for instance, we had never tasted dates. We kept right on chatting and eating until we were ready to burst. Then Lidia and Ester hurried off, for fear that Ermilo might come catch us in that orgy.

Sitting in the vestibule, I waited for Ermilo to come home; I didn't know what to do with myself.

When he arrived, he didn't seem surprised at the change he saw in me. He kissed me on the cheek and said softly: "How lovely you look, my little one."

He gave orders for dinner to be served, not in the big dining room but in a little room with a round table. He nonchalantly took my arm and led me to the table, seating me in the little chair. As the dishes were placed before me, I rejected them one by one, and when he insisted that I eat something, I said dryly: "I'm just not hungry." He didn't insist. There was an awkward silence. As he drank his coffee, he watched me closely and asked:

"What did you tell your mother?"

"Not a thing."

"Well, as a matter of fact she stopped by the grocery store, in tears, completely beside herself, acting like she wanted to apologize for something. But either she didn't know how to make herself clear or I didn't understand her. I had never seen her like that. The only part I got was that she had been by here and thought you were acting strange. What did she mean, *strange*?"

"Well, I'm married now and I've stopped being a momma's girl."

"That's fine, but you should indulge her, spoil her a little."

"Don't you do that *for* me?" I saw his eyes cloud over. Finally, regaining his steely composure, he said:

"Let's go into the library. There are some things you have to do." The library behind Ermilo's office was enormous.

"You see all these books? You don't have to read them all but you should read most of them. We'll begin with historical works that you can quickly absorb. Today, for example, you'll sit here and read everything there is to know about Henry VIII of England and his wives. Just pull on this cord if you want anything. But you can't get up until you're finished. I'll be balancing the books in the office, in case you have any questions. You can look up any words you don't know in those books over there, which are dictionaries. But, like I said, if there's anything you don't understand, just ask."

I swore that I wouldn't ask. I felt deeply offended, humiliated, by that closely guarded prison. Consuelo and Ana would be coming to visit me that afternoon and I told him so. He answered dryly: "We'll just tell them, 'The Señora is busy; she can't receive you today, but she'll send you an invitation to come visit her some other time.' It's all taken care of; I'll tell Simón."

I kicked the enormous globe of the world nearly to pieces. Ermilo must have heard the crash of the books falling, but he pretended he didn't.

At last, completely exhausted, I took off my shoes and started reading about the loves of Henry VIII. I have to admit that I started to enjoy it. At the end of the afternoon, a servant came in with a candelabra, which he placed at my side, together with a cold drink. More hours went by before Ermilo opened the door and asked:

"Have you finished?"

"Yes."

"Then we can have supper."

This time we ate in the great dining room, without exchanging a word. That night, after brushing my hair, instead of putting on my nightgown, Eloísa started dressing me and fixing my hair extravagantly, as if I were going to a masked ball:

"What's the meaning of this, Eloísa?"

"It's the señor's orders," she answered solemnly. Then she took me to the master bedroom and left me there alone.

The minutes slowly, very slowly passed, until Ermilo appeared, with his big belly, dressed in a king's robes and crown. I recognized him from an engraving that I had seen that afternoon; he was Henry VIII. I greeted him with a hearty laugh.

"What a wonderful idea! I've never been to a masked ball before."

"Silence! This is serious! Let's see if you learned today's lesson; you're Anne Boleyn. And he started reciting words and verses of love to me, while he chased me around the room with his arms outstretched. "Now we've come to the act of love. Let's do it, my dear. It will give us both pleasure, since we're in love with one other. Then we'll continue with the story."

As he approached me, I threw a Chinese vase at him. The vase shattered on his head and knocked the royal crown off. His forehead began to bleed. I felt frightened.

"Adulteress, degenerate, heretic! You're condemned to die." And he took a little knife out of his robes; I could see it gleaming in the candlelight. But blood clouded his vision. I managed to reach the door; it was locked. He wiped his face with a sheet and, ripping off a strip, he wrapped it around his forehead.

"This time you'll pay with your blood!" he shouted. I was petrified. His hand caught me, but by ripping my dress I managed to get away, and we went on like that, with him trying to grab me with his hands, with his fingernails, and with me running away, forever running away. Until he finally trapped me in front of the fireplace. We were both out of breath and we stood there glaring with hatred at each other. Then he grabbed me roughly by the neck and made me get down on my hands and knees. "This is where you'll die." And to frighten me even more, he cut the clothes off my back with the back of the knife, and sank it into my flesh.

He shuddered, carefully picked me up off the floor, and said, "Well, what option did I have? I must be mad, my angel." He pressed me to his chest. I was panting. He calmed me down little by little, running his hands over my half-naked body. Then he began to caress me and, suddenly, he held me by my braid and kissed me; he stuck his enormous tongue into my mouth and I felt like his thick saliva was drowning me. My repugnance was stronger than my fear of death and, when I finally managed to break loose, I spit out his saliva.

"I'd rather die right here and now than have you kiss me that way again."

Contrary to my expectations, he pulled himself away from me, ashamed, and said quietly: "It won't happen again. But you,

you . . . what have I done to you tonight?" He got down on his hands and knees and finished removing the shreds of clothing still clinging to my body. Taking me in his arms, he carried me to the master bed, sprinkled with his blood. With his fingertips barely touching me, he murmured over and over, "My beauty, my beauty, my beauty . . . " until I fell asleep.

"My God! What is this!" exclaimed Eloísa when she saw me lying on the bloody bed.

"It's nothing, nothing at all," I reassured her.

"Nothing? And how about the doctor the señor sent for early this morning? Nothing, and here you are all beat up like this, covered with scratches and with a wound running down your back?"

"A nice warm bath will take care of everything."

"A bath?"

"Yes, I'm exhausted and sticky all over. All I want is a bath, my dear Eloísa. And you're going to draw it for me, right now."

"As the señora wishes."

She went off muttering to herself and I tried to sit up. It was so painful! I felt like there wasn't an unfractured bone or unbroken patch of skin in my body. One of my feet was crushed, my elbows and knees were bloodied, there were scratches all over my body and face. Then I did jump up to look in the mirror: my face was bruised and battered. My pallor wasn't caused by rage but by pain.

When I sank into the warm tub I felt a great sense of relief, and afterward, when Eloísa put arnica on my bruises and a magnificent ointment on my wounds, I felt much better.

"The doctor is waiting for you in the sitting room."

"And he'll see me naked; no, it's better that I not see him."

"But ma'am, your husband sent for him; your wound has to be tended . . . "

"Eloísa, don't you let anyone come in here, not a soul. You just bring me my meals. Tell them I have a contagious disease and that the doctor won't allow visitors. Oh! And when Lidia and Ester get here, show them into the game room and serve them sherbet. Bring me some, too."

"Yes, ma'am." And seeing me haggard, collapsed onto the

divan, she looked very sad and went away so she wouldn't bother me.

I didn't finish breakfast, because my mother shot into my sitting room like a cannonball.

"My daughter sick? And I can't see her? This is an affront to God! Even if I catch it, even if I die, it's my duty to be at her bedside. And who are you, Eloísa, to stop me? Neither you nor the doctor nor any other living soul. It's my sacred duty . . . "

She was shouting so loud that I thought my aching head would split.

"Go away, Mother; I'm in the best of care and your screams will just make me worse. Come back in two weeks, like the doctor said. Please stop shouting now.

Two weeks is a short and a very long time. My mother would come over every day and, huddled against the door of my sitting room, she would weep softly and moan. That made me realize that she must have sold me knowing full well about Ermilo's licentious lifestyle, which he didn't try to hide. Little by little, Eloísa told me about his escapades in the neighboring towns, and she said no one in the big house expected him to ever get married, much less to a young girl like me. As she reached the end of each story, Eloísa would burst into sobs.

After two weeks had gone by, my mother appeared with all the usual fanfare, shouts, and threats.

I had a splitting headache and my stitches, which were infected, had turned into open wounds. I had sent word to Ermilo to call a doctor. Furthermore, I felt very weak.

As best I could, I reached the sitting room and opened the door. I stood in the doorway, unbuttoned my robe and let it fall to the floor.

"Want to see more?" and I turned my back on her.

"How was that bastard capable of ?. . ."

"Shut up, Mother. You married me off to that bastard and I live with him here in this house, where you can't talk about him that way. He supports you and even pays for your maid. It wouldn't do for anyone to know that. Get this into your head: I'm the victim of a painful, contagious illness and can't have any visitors. Not even you, because you hurt me."

Shunning her tears, I returned to my divan without picking up the robe. Eloísa shut the door. She brought me another robe and left me alone to rest.

In the afternoon, I sent a message to Ermilo, inquiring how he was and asking him to send me some books he thought I should read.

He brought them himself and, down on his hands and knees before my divan, he begged me over and over again to forgive him, all the while kissing my bruised hands.

He was wearing a tall ostrich-feather hat that was out of season. His face was red and swollen. But neither of us said a word about our wounds. From that day on, we made a silent pact in which I indulged his fantasies now and then and he strictly observed my prohibitions, and you could say we were happy for over twenty years.

I learned how to ride horseback in order to make the rounds of Ermilo's most distant properties. I also learned the workings of the store, how to handle the payroll, how to keep the books; in short, everything a shop owner could learn. We didn't have any children.

Every so often, rumors would reach me that Ermilo had gone on a drunken spree in a neighboring town. I pretended not to hear. But the unrestrained orgy that took place when he turned sixty-eight seemed like an affront to me, because it was right there, in town, in a camp where the gypsies gladly took off their clothes and let themselves be felt up. It was even said that he had shared the bed of the youngest gypsy man. They were all handsomely paid, to their great satisfaction. The party lasted for three days.

Very early on the fourth day, I was preparing to go to our property, La Esmeralda, when someone banged on the door. Simón went to open it and I stood there waiting to see who it was. I could hear Simón arguing with someone.

"Let him in," I ordered.

A tall man walked in; I couldn't make out his face because Ermilo's belly protruded from the man's shoulders and Ermilo's head hung over his back.

"Put him down on the floor," I ordered, and I had to turn my head and cover my mouth to keep from vomiting at such filth.

"Would you kindly carry him upstairs, since he's too heavy for me to handle, and once he's in his room you can leave him to Simón. Oh! You can take a bath up there, and I'll have them bring you a clean change of clothes," I said with my back to the man.

I ordered a cup of tea to calm my stomach.

How can I put it? I saw him standing there at the top of the stairs: strong, blond, agile, sure of his movements and with an arrogant air that reminded me of some engraving—Achilles! He was the most beautiful living being I had ever laid eyes on.

My mouth tasted like honey.

He came toward me and his blue eyes filled my soul with light. I had to sit down.

"I've followed madam's instructions and I'm obliged for this magnificent outfit."

"Quiet, quiet. It's we who are obliged, and I couldn't possibly repay you for the good turn you have done us."

"—The poor man . . . no one wanted to go near him . . . someone told me his name and where he lived, and I brought him home. Anyone can have a stroke of bad luck."

"But this wasn't bad luck and you know it."

His eyes met mine:

"There are different kinds of bad luck," he said, very self-assured.

"I'd like you to join me for breakfast if you would be so kind."

"The kindness is yours and it wouldn't be proper—"

"In this house I decide what's proper and what isn't."

"I'm at your command."

I was giving him orders, when what I wanted was to be his slave.

During breakfast, he told me that his name was Simpson, since his father had been an Englishman. His mother was Mexican, but when he was twelve years old, his father had gotten it into his head that he should join the British merchant marine. They both went to Europe to join up. As a sailor's apprentice Simpson was a flop, and he told me some salty stories that made me roar with laughter, something that I hadn't done in years and that made the servants nervous.

"I want you to go with me to La Esmeralda; you can make yourself useful."

"As the señora wishes . . . but I have to return the hay wagon that I brought the señor home in. A good-hearted stranger loaned it to me."

"You go ahead, I still have some things to take care of here."

Of course, it was a lie, and I spent the time dolling myself up. I sang, and Eloísa made fun of me because two out of three notes were off-key. But I didn't care.

"Is the señora happy because the señor has come home?"

I stopped cold.

"Yes, Eloísa . . . and go tell them to saddle up the chestnut and the sorrel."

Eloísa left and I sank into a pool of pain. Simpson must be twenty-three or twenty-four, and I was tied to Ermilo and was thirty-six, though I didn't look it by a long shot. But what was happening? Was that desire to laugh and feel happy a sin? Yet I knew deep down that I was lying to myself, that it was Simpson, Simpson who made me a stranger to myself.

Very calm, trying to look majestic, I slowly descended the stairs when they announced that "the young man had returned." I nodded to him and the feather hanging from my little hat trembled slightly, as if it were mocking me.

"Let's go," I said authoritatively. He followed. He followed me down the road without uttering a word or asking what we were going to do, what he was going to do.

Before we reached La Esmeralda, I reined my horse in alongside his and asked him point-blank:

"Do you want a job? Do you know anything about farmwork?"

"Very little, but I'm a fast learner."

"Good." And, whipping my horse, I rode away from him again. It wasn't easy!

At the sound of the horses, Jerónimo came limping out of his shack and, when he saw me, he knelt down on the ground.

I reined in my horse and, before I knew what was happening, Simpson's strong hands lifted me by the waist and placed me on the ground.

"Don't ever do that again," I told him brusquely.

Jerónimo, with his arm and leg bandaged, was shouting, "The señora has arrived! The señora! She's come to see me!"

"That's why I'm here, to bring you some help," I told him haughtily. "Let's go inside and have a look at those wounds."

"I was careless, señora, I blinked."

"Be quiet now and let me have a look at you." I began gingerly removing the dirty rags and saw with horror the deep, infected wounds.

"Bring in the saddlebags," I ordered Simpson. He complied.

I began to tend the wound with the greatest of care. I thoroughly disinfected it; Jerónimo's face twisted and he bit his lips so as not to yell out. Simpson held him up. Jerónimo fainted and then I was able to tend to him more easily and efficiently.

"It's a good thing he doesn't have a fever," Simpson said.

"Well, if we don't get him to town, he'll not only have a fever, we'll have to amputate."

"No, not that!" he shouted, "And now we don't have anything to carry him back in, in his weakened condition. I'll stay here and take care of him until he's strong as an oak. I know how to do it. You learn a lot of things at sea. And I can hunt for our food."

"That won't be necessary. I'll come back myself or send you whatever you need. You do know how to write, don't you? Write me notes letting me know what you need, what both of you need."

After Jerónimo came to, we ate "angel's breasts," as he called them, and we gave him rather more to drink than we needed to.

When I got back home I turned the matter over to Fulgencio, the field boss, and I went about my life as usual.

I didn't see Ermilo for two weeks; I found out he had called a doctor, and that gave me an opportunity.

I couldn't bear to stay home, so I visited Santa Prisca, El Matorral, La Acequia, but the chestnut strayed. As dusk was falling, we reached La Esmeralda to check on the patient. He was getting better by the hour, and since it was getting late, Simpson escorted me home on horseback, telling me his stories. How disappointed I was to see the town lights in the distance.

"See you later."

"See you later, señora."

And it occurred to me that I had been on the verge of saying, "I'll never see you again, Simpson."

That was my intention when I decided to stopped going out there.

After a tearful, contrite reunion, Ermilo and I went on with our life as usual, the life we had molded out of so many years of living together, except now we had no sexual contact.

One day, Ermilo went out dressed in his field clothes but in a horsedrawn cart; he didn't ride horseback anymore. "He must be going to inspect some property," I thought.

When he came back that afternoon he looked healthier than ever, radiant. He called me into the library.

"We'll be as rich as Croesus! And you hadn't breathed a word about that Mr. Simpson; he'll make us multimillionaires! What would you like? Samarcand? The Persian Gulf? Tripoli? Madagascar? China? Japan? Tonkin? Korea? ... He has it all in the palm of his hand. He worked for years in the English merchant navy and has hundreds of contacts, and he knows the routes, the shipping companies. And of course, he speaks fluent English and can handle the correspondence. Now we won't be merchants, but distributors ... and you leave him in charge of taking care of Jerónimo, ha, ha, ha!"

I could foresee Simpson collaborating with us, and exclaimed fearfully:

"What do we need so much money for? We already have more than we could possibly spend in our lifetimes, with enough left over to travel around the world and bequeath a fortune to needy families."

"But don't you know what power money can buy you?"

"No."

"It can buy other people's humiliation."

Simpson started working himself to the bone at the store. He slept in a room on the mezzanine in the same wing of the house where our bedrooms were, but he wouldn't get home at night until we were asleep.

It would be an exaggeration to say that I slept, because from the moment Simpson arrived I could barely shut my eyes. I went to see the doctor, who, without asking the cause of my insomnia—he knew Ermilo as well as anyone—gave me a little bottle and told me to take five drops each night. That way I managed to fall asleep once I heard Simpson lock up the house for the night. Then his footsteps, and at last, silence.

When the wonders of the Orient began to arrive, I had to go admire them at the store. But all I could see were Simpson's elastic movements as he showed them to me. Ermilo was there.

"Pick something . . . anything that strikes your fancy," he egged me on.

But the only thing I could see were Simpson's eyes. He weighed me down with cloths, perfume, objects, carefully explaining where they had come from. I would accept them because they came from his hands. When several shipments had arrived, Ermilo organized a great exhibition at our house and invited all the well-to-do merchants of the region. The buyers slept over in the southern wing of the house.

Business was booming.

That night, after the exhibition was taken down, we gave a grand ball.

Sordidly, hidden in the corner of a balcony, I watched how the women chased Simpson. He could have his pick of any of them for his lover or wife, but Simpson seemed not to notice. He was gracious with them all but not with anyone in particular.

When I saw that, I left my hiding place and mingled with the guests.

My childhood friends surrounded me:

"Tomorrow we'll come see your treasures."

"And by the way, your business partner is gorgeous."

"And nice . . ."

Toward the end of the party, I started drinking champagne. Lots of champagne, until Simpson carried me to my room and covered me with a comforter.

The moon is soiled by black clouds. I light the candle and the shadows of objects pounce on me, making me even more fearful. Everything blames me for my suffering; I understand that my fear is nothing but remorse in disguise, that my beloved objects reject me in disgust because of feeling the love I feel. My love, though, isn't as shaky as I am. I throw the olive-green cape over myself and, without thinking, I wander the corridors and stairways like a sleepwalker, in turn stumbling and staggering. I open the door of Simpson's room. What I see leaves me petrified: Simpson and Ermilo making love.

But I have no time to break out of my stupor. Ermilo has shut the door and is shouting like a man possessed.

"I told you she'd come someday . . . that she'd come . . . she's crazy about you."

He pulls off my cloak and tears off my clothes.

"You'll see what a beauty she is, this daughter of . . . you'll see what a beauty."

While he clumsily undresses me, Simpson goes down on his knees before me, kisses my hand, and says very gently, "Mi señora." I gaze into his childlike eyes and forget all about what I have just seen.

I am naked. Ermilo jumps up and down on his short, skinny legs.

"Now I've got you! Now I've got you!" he shouts at the top of his lungs. "Go climb onto the bearskin, so the fire will cast reflections on your skin!" And he takes out his belt and starts snapping it on the floor.

"Hurry up, lovers, it's getting late!"

Milk and honey under his delicate tongue. Delight in my fingertips when I touch his skin. Simpson runs up and down my body with his hands, with his open mouth. It is so slow and at the same time frantic. It seems as if both of us have waited forever for this encounter. We rest a while so we can gaze at one another with boundless love, and then we caress each other once again, as if eternity had been made for this. When he possesses me, I draw on some unknown experience and start moving rhythmically. Following a long, very long ritual, we lie exhausted on top of each other, lightly caressing each other's bodies with infinite tenderness.

It's then that I realize that Ermilo has been watching us all the while, whipping a large belt and muttering dirty words. I don't care.

We sit up at the snap of Ermilo's belt.

"That's fine, children, fine. You didn't know what this was like, did you, my dear? But now you'll know that and much more."

He hands us champagne glasses. We sit up and my nakedness makes me uncomfortable. He pours more champagne, another glass, another, and yet another . . . how many? He chatters on: "Don't call him Simpson; his first name is Samuel." "Since we're going to be even more intimate friends, starting tomorrow we'll party in your bedroom, which is much lovelier than this one." "Oh, Samuel! You understand both men and women so well!" I'm not sure how much time has gone by, nor do I care what Ermilo is saying. I hide my happiness behind the glasses of champagne. But it isn't the alcohol that makes me drunk: it is Samuel's love; it is the pleasure he has known how to give me.

At some point, Ermilo snaps his belt for the umpteenth time.

"That's enough resting. Now all three of us will have a good time. And I'll be the first one to mount her. OK, Samuel?"

I cringe in horror, but I am already inside the infernal and glorious circle: I have accepted it.

The next day at noon I wake up with a headache, and Eloísa chides me for having drunk too much champagne. She goes to the kitchen to bring me a potion for my nausea. I ask her not to open the curtains.

I lie still, torn by contradictory emotions. I have behaved like a shameless woman, a woman without scruples. What bothers me is sharing my pleasure with Ermilo, whom I detest from this moment on. And sharing my body with two men makes me feel profoundly ashamed: whoever the men might be. But the pleasure I share with Samuel, and the gentle, affectionate caresses that he lavished on me while we were with Ermilo . . . my flesh burns with desire once more, and I feel like I would do it again a thousand times, as long as I could lie in Samuel's arms for a moment. His name is Samuel, now; he's no longer Mr. Simpson. And on the other hand, Ermilo has not only allowed it, he has encouraged it. Despite his disgusting caresses, I tell myself that, in the past, I have had to put up with them just the same, with no accomplice to not only mitigate them but erase them with caresses of his own. All this runs through my mind, but I feel bad morally, physically, and I pull the sheet up over my face: "You're wearing a shroud, dear," Ermilo had told me the morning after our wedding. . . . But no, I was no longer wearing a shroud for the old geezer; I was alive, very much alive with my love for Samuel.

After drinking the horrible brew that Eloísa had concocted, I feel much better. But the curtains are still drawn, since I don't want to face the sun. The sun and I can no longer be friends. I now belong to the sinister, waning moon.

I bathe very slowly and Eloísa gets a little cross with my clumsy, halfhearted movements. She can't persuade me to eat a bite. I ask her to leave me alone there, in my robe.

The struggle within me continues. It isn't easy to forget the principles of a lifetime, no matter how much justification and love there may be on the other side. What would my mother or girlfriends think if they knew what had happened? The same thing I would have thought just a few months ago: nothing, I wouldn't have understood it; I would have been completely scandalized; and I would have called a woman who would do such things depraved, at the very least. But Samuel, Samuel . . . surely neither my mother nor girlfriends has ever dreamed of such a love.

Eloísa came in with a package that had arrived for me from the store. I waited till she left to open it: it was a set of rubies, with a card reading: "My love is greater than yours because, in order to have you, I have had to shed red tears of humiliation in your name. Samuel."

A little while later, a smaller package arrived with a ring to match the rubies: "For the loveliest whore I've ever known. Ermilo." They were in cahoots. Eloísa came in to tell me that the señor and Mr. Simpson were coming to dinner and that I must get dressed immediately. I refused. I sent word that I would expect them for supper. I was the one calling the shots in all this.

That afternoon I gladly entertained my girlfriends, who had come to see "my wonders." Nothing impressed them like my set of rubies. We chatted and ate sweets until late afternoon.

That night, I put on a low-cut black gown and the rubies. Eloísa was confused, because I had never had her dress me with such care, not even for the ball the day before. I descended the stairs, triumphant. Both men outdid each other with compliments.

While we ate, Simpson and I made no pretense of disguising our longing looks, and time and again his hands brushed against mine. When we had finished, Ermilo asked me if the fire was lit in my bedroom; he ordered it to be lit and for the liqueurs and champagne to be sent up to my room. The servants were stunned.

"I'm very fond of that room, and now that Mr. Simpson is part of the family, it shouldn't surprise you if we all have a drink together up there now and again. By the warmth of the fireside. Oh! and by the way, from now on all your salaries will be doubled."

The scene from the previous night was repeated, down to the last detail, but more peaceably, since Ermilo didn't have to rip my clothes off; rather, Samuel slowly undressed me amid embraces and passionate kisses. Ermilo snapped his belt like a lion tamer and was truly desperate to get into the act.

The servants did not keep quiet, as Ermilo had supposed they would when he gave them such fabulous salaries. The whole town found out that something strange was happening in our house, and everyone had their suspicions about what it might be.

As is often the case, my mother was the last one to get wind of the gossip. Since she didn't want to bring up the subject with me in private, one morning she showed up with Father Ochoa, a discreet man for whom I had great respect.

She started by broaching the subject of the scandal.

"We rich folks are eccentric, Father; my husband was already eccentric before we got married and no one warned me about it. And, Father, God is the only one who can truly see what happens, why it happens, and who will look into our hearts. I will respect your judgment."

With this and a few more skirmishes, the interview ended.

But my mother started losing weight, growing pallid, and she soon died.

As her corpse was lowered into the grave, someone shouted:

"Murderess!"

And right afterward a rock struck me in the forehead.

Ermilo shouted: "Stop it! I saw you throw that rock, Ascensión Rodríguez! This very afternoon you'll hear from my lawyers. From now on anyone who offends my wife in any way, their account at the store will be payable in full, if they don't want their property confiscated."

In addition to my guilt for bringing on my mother's death, I still have the scar on my forehead as a continual reminder.

I would ride horseback every day, tend the flowers in the garden, just to keep in shape. Eloísa, who was growing ever more silent, would cover my body with cool masks of fruit, creams, delicate oils. I would pamper my body all day long, so that it wouldn't wither, so it would look and feel desirable each night. I tried not to think about anything but Samuel, because if I read, or if my thoughts dwelt on reality, I would start to lose my precarious equilibrium. Above all, I must not think about aging or the future. All that existed was each day, for the sake of each night.

But someone did think about my future: Ermilo. He made out a will stipulating that Mr. Samuel Simpson should not marry or cohabit with any woman except me, his beloved wife, and if this clause was not observed, the partnership would be dissolved in terms very unfavorable to Simpson. On the other hand, when I died he would be the sole heir to our entire fortune. Samuel, laughing, accepted the terms and swore he would never leave me.

Our orgies continued night after night, although in the end Ermilo participated only to a very limited extent.

Ermilo died at age eighty-five. I was fifty-three and Samuel barely forty. Despite my youthful appearance, when I found myself alone with Simpson, without Ermilo's support—I only realized now that he had given me support—I was filled with a terror that made my teeth chatter. Why didn't I trust Samuel? During all those years he had been so loving toward me that I should feel certain his passion was as intense as mine, but now I was afraid of my sweet Samuel. Why?

We would eat alone in the immense dining room and the conversation would lag. At supper I would be nervous, vigilant, but the days went by, ending in nights with a kiss on the hand and a "Sleep well." Of course, I didn't sleep. In my desperation, I begged Ermilo, as if he were a saint, to intercede on my behalf, not to abandon me.

And my prayers were answered. Ten days after Ermilo's death, as we finished supper, Samuel took my hand and we went up to the bedroom. Oh! I was so happy! Alone, with no witnesses. At last! We could become one or be one person inside the other. How can I describe our caresses? We invented them all, because there had never been any lovers in the world before us. Exhausted, we watched the sunrise, but the sun clouded over when Samuel took me by the hand and said: "I miss Ermilo."

Those were lazy days and burning nights. I would go from the bed to the bath and from the bath to the divan slowly, savoring my movements, the sweet warmth of the water, Eloísa's smile, the caress of my silk clothes, the perfumes of the late morning. I felt as if I were recuperating from an illness that had placed my life in danger, and I pampered myself delicately. I would fall asleep remembering the previous night's words of love, and would sleep gently, as if wrapped in a cocoon. I didn't go down to dinner, because those days Samuel wasn't eating at home, but the ritual of dressing for supper would begin at six in the afternoon, since it was necessary to disguise, cover up, trap, and tame the least wrinkle on my face, my hands, all over my body, and to bring out the glow of beauty in all its plenitude. I was aware of my age but he wasn't and, if the truth be told, I still looked much younger than I was. And beautiful, I was still very beautiful. He never tired of telling me so.

How long did the spell last? Weeks? Months? I don't know, because I didn't bother keeping track of time, since I dwelt in eternity, a fleeting eternity.

I started to worry when he began repeating every night that we needed Ermilo, that everything had been better when he was around, that he missed Ermilo. I felt wounded but couldn't bring myself to say so.

One night, he asked me very gallantly if I would mind if he brought a friend to supper, saying "We're so alone," and that I could pick the day, plan the menu; that he was leaving everything in my hands. I didn't like the idea of having our intimacy invaded, but I could think of no way to argue against such a natural thing. We set the date and didn't speak about the supper or his friend again. I should have been more curious, should have inquired about him and what sort of friend he was, but, no doubt in self-defense, I forgot all about it until the evening before.

I laid the table with the best linen, brought out the silver, and ordered an exquisite menu. I dressed with greater care than ever before and waited.

Contrary to etiquette, when Samuel arrived with his friend, I stood up to greet them. The friend was a very young, blond man with a ridiculous moustache. He seemed very self-satisfied. As he stood before me, he poked out his chin and made an almost military bow. I nearly laughed, but was dumbfounded when Samuel said,

"Laura, this is ... well, to simplify things we'll call him Ermilo; do you mind?"

I understood immediately and agreed.

That Ermilo, whom I didn't like, was followed by many, many Ermilos, and there ensued the famous orgies of the Ermilos, in which I was the main attraction, since I was the only woman. When I started aging and losing my teeth, getting wrinkled, ugly, I began to attract more important personages, those who had desired me when I was young, and young men wanting to enjoy a beauty goddess. All the founding fathers of the city had dealings with me in those orgies, which, fortunately, weren't all that frequent. It was they who took back to town scandalous tales about the goings-on at my house.

My house ... or what is left of it. Looted by the Ermilos, with Samuel's consent, the curtains ripped to shreds, the rugs stolen, the furniture rickety and soiled, reeking of semen and vomit, it's more like a pigsty than a home, but it's the appropriate setting for me, and that's how Samuel likes it.

I'm now seventy-two. He's barely fifty-nine. I don't have any teeth left; I can only suck, and I no longer make any attempt to conceal my age. But Samuel loves me; there can be no doubt about that. Following orgies where they rip me apart, wound me, unleash their most abject and ferocious fantasies on me, Samuel tucks me into bed and comforts me with untold tenderness; he bathes me and tends to me as to a prized possession. Once I'm feeling better, and taking advantage of my convalescence, we make love all by ourselves. He kisses my toothless, lipless mouth, with the same passion as the first time, and I feel happy once again. My soul is blooming like it should have bloomed when I was young. I've renounced everything for the sake of these torrid springs, overflowing with love, and I believe God understands. That's why I'm not the least bit afraid of death.